ROBINSON CRUSOE

My Journals and Sketchbooks

ROBINSON CRUSOE

My Journals and Sketchbooks

HARCOURT BRACE JOVANOVICH

New York and London

A REMARKABLE FIND?

"Today, the seventh May 1684, I. Robinson Crusoe, once master and sole inhabitant of a lost island, here bring to an end my sketchbooks and my journal, in which for almost a quarter of a century I have told and pictured my strange adventures. May the story of my fortune set dreaming those who have the soul of a wanderer. Robinson Crusoe."

So ends the incredible manuscript which a stranger has just placed on my desk. This is how it happened. One dull day in the winter of 1966 I was only paying absent-minded attention to the entrance of a visitor, Michel Politzer, who came as if it were the simplest thing in the world to offer me the discovery of the century. Thinking myself to be dealing with a simple dreamer, I prepared to see him out politely, but he guessed my intention:

"One day you will certainly be sorry, sir, if you refuse to listen to me now, because what I have in this case is a find as important as was in its own day the discovery of Tutankhamen's tomb."

Amused by such an assertion, I invited my visitor to explain his meaning in more detail. "Here, my dear sir, is what I suggest that you publish." And he opened his case. At once the sour smell, the lasting stink of he-goat, mixed with as strong a scent of mildew, invaded the room. My visitor, not at all concerned, laid out before me some scraps of goatskin, as stiff as bits of bark. Taking refuge by the window I glanced sideways at my desk where this crude debris was spread, but apart from the smell there appeared nothing remarkable, nothing anyway worth publishing. And worse still, I had before me a visitor hard to get rid of. Unruffled, he proceeded.

Copyright © 1972 by Editions Joël Cuénot

Translation copyright © 1974 by André Deutsch Limited
All rights reserved.

Based on the book *Robinson Crusoe* by Daniel Defoe
Originally published in France by Editions Joël Cuénot under
the title of *Robinson Crusoé: mes carnets de croquis*

First American edition 1974
Printed in Great Britain

Library of Congress Cataloging in Publication Data

[Politzer, Anie]
   My journals and sketchbooks.

   SUMMARY: Many of Robinson Crusoe's adventures, told in his "own" words,
illustrated with his "own" sketches as recorded in his journal and sketchbook
supposedly unearthed years later in an old Scottish manor house.
   Text by Anie Politzer; drawings by Michel Politzer.
   Translation of Mes carnets de croquis.
   Presented as a newly-discovered sketchbook by Daniel Defoe's fictional character,
Robinson Crusoe.
   [1.   Survival–Fiction. 2.   Shipwrecks–Fiction] I.   Politzer, Michel, illus.
II.   Defoe, Daniel, 1661?–1731. Robinson Crusoe.   III   Title.
PZ7.P754My   [Fic]   74-2240
ISBN 0–15–267836–0

"At first sight, these documents" (he stressed the word "documents") "tell you nothing. Nevertheless, there on your desk you have the authentic drawings made by Robinson Crusoe himself on his island."

"But Robinson Crusoe is a character in fiction, born of the imagination of Daniel Defoe!"

"That is what I believed for a long time, like everyone else. But one day a strange thing happened." Here Michel Politzer lowered himself into a chair. "Believe it or not, my wife has inherited from a great-grand-uncle an old manor in Scotland. When we came to take possession of this ancient house, we found at the bottom of a chest left in the innermost corner of an attic, a large and carefully wrapped parcel . . . And in this parcel . . ."

"In this parcel you have presumably found the drawings and manuscript which you are showing me. And what then? What did you do?"

"We began at once to examine our discovery. Being myself an artist, I was naturally chiefly concerned with the restoration of the drawings, while my wife Anie applied herself to transcribing the manuscript. See here." He held out a fragment of dry yellowed parchment on which a few marks were barely visible.

"The drawing itself is practically illegible, but if it is photographed, using special film and filters, you get this." Michel Politzer then took out of his papers a large photograph which showed a tent placed against a cliff and surrounded by a palisade. Suddenly, as if by magic, the smell had disappeared! I was, I admit, a little stirred by this. My interviewer showed me one after another of these big photographs, reproductions of fine drawings. All the adventures of the Robinson Crusoe of my youth passed before my eyes!

"Finally," my visitor continued, "we got in touch with several publishers, but not one would publish our discovery! Do you know why?"

"They told you that you were so impassioned a lover of Defoe's novel that you had allowed yourself to imagine that you yourself were Robinson Crusoe!"

"Exactly, you see it all! I certainly admit that this story enchanted my childhood and enthrals me still," Michel Politzer shrewdly replied.

It must be acknowledged that the drawings are remarkable, sometimes most affecting; they tell as never before the story of a man alone, living happily in the midst of wild nature.

And after all, dear reader, is it necessary before publishing a story to be persuaded of its truth? Is it not better, if the story is a fine one, to let oneself be convinced, and to believe, even for a moment, that Robinson Crusoe really existed?

André Deutsch

POOR ROBINSON CRUSOE!

Ought I to praise or blame Heaven for having saved my life from the terrible shipwreck which, two days ago, cast me up alone on this unknown coast? All my shipmates and my dear captain were drowned in this frightful tempest, all were lost! Here am I, a rich sugar-cane planter of Brazil, condemned to the most complete solitude, reduced to the fate of a starving and shivering savage, overcome by this horror. I am shipwrecked, cast up on a land doubtless swarming with fierce beasts and cannibals. Alas! Alas! What will become of me?

3 OCTOBER 1659

I wrote those despairing words while prey to the stormiest emotions. As soon as I had dashed them on to paper I felt a little quietened, as if I had confided in a friend. I shall note down from day to day the turns of fortune which agitate my present life, as much to forget nothing of these extraordinary events as to comfort my anguished soul. Indeed, my situation is not to be envied, as I take up my pen today, leaning my elbow on an old seachest, aching with hunger and barely sheltered from the rain under a miserable scrap of canvas. But I should be ungrateful to Providence if I did not say at once that, on the day after the shipwreck, our vessel having run aground some cable lengths from the shore, I was able to bring back cases of provisions, arms and various utensils. I had the luck also to find the ship's log, on the blank pages of which I am now writing, and on which I have made this sketch of our poor wrecked ship.

I read on the last page of the log, written by our worthy captain, under the date of 29 September 1659:
Stormy weather – Visibility reduced – 7°22′ Latitude N.
and under the date of 30 September:
Tempest – Visibility nil – no check on latitude. Mizzen mast smashed. GOD SAVE OUR SOULS.
Below the captain's entry (may he rest in peace) I add that on the 30 September at 16 hours a fearful whirlwind staved in the bulwarks to port and snapped the foremast across. At this moment a sailor cried out, "Land ahead!" A violent shock flung us on the deck. The ship was breaking up on a sandbank. The captain and crew, certain that the vessel was sinking, launched the ship's boat, and we embarked, commending our souls to God. At the first breaker the boat capsized and I was swallowed up by the waves. I had to struggle a long time, in the grasp of unspeakable terror, before I could draw breath again and swim a little. Not far off I saw a dark coast and boldly I swam towards it. But I was dashed against a jutting rock with such force that the shock made me lose consciousness for a few seconds. I held on hard, gripping with the little strength I had left; it was this rock that saved my life. For I waited there, numb, shivering, but out of the water, until the squall moved off; and then, in a calm period, I reached the shore by swimming. I climbed over the rocks on the beach and collapsed on the grass. Then I ran about, throwing up my arms and crying out with joy to find myself safe and sound.
After this moment of exaltation I was struck by a feeling of shocking loneliness. In vain I shouted, searched the rocks, gazed at the black water; no one answered my cries. I was

alone; the only one rescued from the disaster. And I was very near to losing my reason, for I began to run about weeping like a madman, until I fell fainting on the ground.

When evening came I suddenly thought that, having nothing at all on me but a pipe, a knife and a little tobacco, I would be irrevocably lost if a wild beast appeared, or any other harmful creature. The only resource that came to my mind was to climb a tree and pass the night there. I drank a little water from a stream, ate some fruit, cut myself a thick stick, and climbed into the fork of a great tree where I slept with all the ease in the world. I break off my story here, night coming on me so fast that I can no longer see to write.

4 OCTOBER

When I woke up it was full daylight, and the first thing I saw, at about a mile from the beach, was the ship, which the tide must have lifted from the sandbank and carried to the rocks of which I spoke above. At once I longed to go on board. But I had to wait at least three hours before the tide was low enough. Hunger pinching me, I picked some bananas, but I dared not venture farther into the forest that fringed the shore, for without any weapon but my pocket-knife I would cut a wretched figure facing the terrible dangers which lay in wait for me in this unknown land and which I felt growling in my rear. Was it an island or a continent? Was it peopled by civilized men or hateful savages?

Towards midday, the sea having uncovered a long sandbank, I went out as far as possible towards the ship, whose keel, driven aground, tilted high the deck and bulwarks. I threw off my clothes, keeping only my breeches, and plunged into the sea. When I reached the vessel I had to swim round her twice before I could catch hold of a rope's end which hung from the broken foremast and haul myself up on deck. There my grief was redoubled in realizing that if we had remained on board we would all have been saved. The ship's deck slanted sharply, the stern up and the prow under water, but all the back part was high and dry. I searched there first of all for everything that was intact, and above all for provisions, which I needed most. I went to the bread-store where I filled my pockets with ship's biscuits, and began to eat them while hunting further. Next I needed to find a small boat in which to bring to shore all my findings, but I saw nothing that could serve. I then had the notion of building a raft with the spare yards and masts. So, having found the carpenter's tool-chest, I sawed two mizzen masts to the right size, tied them with ropes and threw them into the sea along with the yards. I climbed down the ship's side to fasten all together with strong ropes. I nailed across this base a solid platform made of planks and placed on top three empty seaman's chests. These I filled with provisions, tools and weapons: in the first, I put bread, rice, three Dutch cheeses, five sides of dried meat and a little mixed wheat and barley.

While I was loading all this, I saw that the tide was rising and to my great distress had carried away the clothes I had left on the sand. I had therefore to hunt for slops and found seamen's clothes of good strong cloth and fitting. The second chest I loaded with tools, planks and ropes, as well as the precious carpenter's chest. Finally, I discovered in the captain's cabin two shotguns, two pistols, four old swords, powder flasks, a bag of shot, a compass, the ship's log, ink and quill pens. I packed all these in the third chest. Night has fallen while I write this long account and I can no longer see. I have lived for five days as a poor castaway. What will tomorrow bring?

SIXTH DAY, ALAS!

I put on board, as well as the third chest, several barrels of gunpowder, and, finding it loaded enough, I took an old oar to steer by and pushed off my raft. The tide rose, the wind blew towards the shore; all went well until half a mile from the beach, when suddenly my raft drifted into a strong current which swept me towards a creek. There, I was on the point of having another shipwreck for my raft hit a sandbank which barred the mouth of the little river: it rocked there half-buried in the sand, and I had to wait a good hour for the rising tide to float me off again. At once I pushed up the channel towards the land: I spied a little cove on the left where after much trouble I was able to strand my raft undamaged. I fastened it to a tree-trunk and began to unload it. When that was done, I took a shotgun, a powder flask and two pistols, and full of courage set out to explore. I soon climbed a high hill, it is hilly country. There my unhappy fate was revealed. I was on an island in the middle of the ocean, and the nearest shores were desert reefs more than four miles away.

When I returned it was almost night; I made myself a sort of hut with the chests and planks and, well barricaded, I passed my second night on this unknown isle. Next day I returned to the ship in order to bring off as many things as possible before it was broken up by rough seas.

EIGHTH DAY

Yesterday I brought back from the ship a quantity of tools, a drill, a dozen hatchets, a grindstone for sharpening, iron crowbars, a large bag of nails and rivets; with sails, ropes, poles, two more barrels of powder, a box of musket balls, seven muskets, a third shotgun, lead, a hammock, a mattress, blankets, clothes and greatcoats. I thought I had rescued nearly all that was on board. But I was wrong, for today, returning from a trip to the wreck that almost cost me dear – the wind having risen, I capsized with my whole load in the middle of the creek – I saw Japp, the captain's dog, come

bounding joyfully along, an Irish setter I had thought drowned with the crew. I think that the poor beast, swept away by the current, had landed on the island much farther away, and had difficulty in finding me. This evening I pitched a little tent with the poles and sail-cloth, under which I spread out my bed. I have piled up all my riches in a shelter from the rain that was threatening. My dog snores at my feet, I have dined on a bit of dried meat and a ship's biscuit, and in spite of the rising wind I am prepared to pass a good night.

TWELFTH DAY PASSED ON THE ISLAND

I was very hungry this morning. It had rained and blown a devilish wind all night and the tent had been partly torn away. But the worst was that, in opening the chest where I had stored my ship's biscuits, I saw that the rain had spoilt my provisions. It was with a very sad heart that I prepared to make a meal off two soaked biscuits. Suddenly, taken with foreboding, I sprang out of the tent and ran to the beach. I all but lost heart: the ship had disappeared, swept away by the night's storm. Now nothing henceforth bound me to my past life. But on reflection I consoled myself by thinking that I had neglected no chance to bring out of the poor hulk everything useful for my subsistence.

I must now guard my life against attacks by wild men, savage animals, and the elements. I recognize that my present camp is neither suited to my safety nor to my liking, for it is in danger of being flooded by high tides, and what is more it has no fresh water. I must find a dry place, sheltered from rain and sun, and easy to protect from enemies of all kinds. It must also be in sight of the sea, for I keep hoping to be rescued by a ship.

This afternoon I have discovered, half a mile from here, a little level plain on a gentle slope at the edge of the shore.

It is sheltered to north and east by a peaked cliff: to the right a river runs into the sea, and will supply, I hope, both water and protection. In the face of the cliff is a cavity where I shall put my bed, and which has also given me the idea of hollowing out a cave for the protection of myself, my weapons and my provisions. Here I am going to set up my home.

A REAL DOWNPOUR

I began to shift my camp, but the rain which started again in the afternoon forced me to erect a temporary tent against the face of the cliff, there to store my most precious goods. Carrying the full chests is very exhausting. I have to make haste between two downpours; and am very glad indeed to have brought back plenty of casks and rolls of sailcloth which I can roll along the ground from one camp to the other, since I have to drag along the boxes and chests laboriously by ropes. I hope to make my tent bigger and to double its space with another roomier one, because rains are frequent in this climate.

Crouched in my tent, I have breakfasted on a bit of dried meat and a biscuit, so heavy were the rainstorms. My thoughts are gloomy, for my provisions are running out; I shall have to hunt for food in the woods. At the moment I am thinking of protecting my dwelling by an enclosure, either a stone wall or a wooden palisade, I do not yet know which. I shall build this wall against the cliff-face in a semicircle round my tent. I shall give this enclosure a radius of at least 45 feet, which seems sufficient. A bright sun is shining just now on sea and land; I must go to finish my house-moving.

FOURTEENTH DAY

It has rained all night, but this morning it is brilliant sunshine. In the forest the bird calls are so loud that I can hardly bear them. I am going off to cut palings, for I have decided to make a wooden palisade. The stones round here are too small, not bigger than my fist, and rounded by the sea. Perhaps I can make throwing stones of them for a sling. Not far from here I have found a wood where a sort of willow grows whose branches are strong and easy to cut. I shall work until night comes.

MY FIRST WORK ON THE ISLAND

I am constructing my palisade by placing the palings, sharpened at the ends, very close together, fastened by ropes, and reinforced, here and there, by other posts leaning against them to act as buttresses. I shall have no door but a ladder to draw up behind me over my rampart. I have forgotten to say that the latter is a good $5\frac{1}{2}$ feet high. Thus, I shall fortify myself, I hope, from the wild beasts of the island; but it is a rough work and clumsy, of which I cannot yet see the end.

MY CALENDAR-POST

It is now already twenty or twenty-two days since I set foot on this island for the first time, half-dead with cold and terror. I thought this morning that I would erect a monument to mark the place and the fatal date of my arrival here. So I drove into the sand a strong post on which I nailed a small board carved with these words: *I landed here 30 September 1659.* As well as noting the most important days in my journal, I shall make a notch each day on my post; the seventh notch longer and the first day of each month longer still. Thus I shall not lose the sense of time passing.

27 OCTOBER/I RETURN FROM A SHORT JOURNEY

It must be said that the heavy work of putting my castle in order, hollowing out my cave more and more deeply because of rains and storms, and putting up my barricade, did not leave me much time for going out, except to hunt. But yesterday a longing took me to explore the extent of my territory, and to make certain that I was the sole occupant. I equipped myself, therefore, with a gun, my pistols, powder flask, and a bag of bread and cheese. I plunged deep into the unknown, my faithful Japp at my side, retracing the course of the stream which entered the sea at the foot of my beach. As soon as I left the heat of the shore I entered into the alarming depths of a forest of great trees where a whole colony of monkeys, birds and strange beasts were moving about in the greatest uproar.

To my annoyance a band of small howling monkeys* surrounded me at once, a noisy following I could well have done without. They even came to bother me when I sat down to eat my dinner; a shot fired in the air served to scatter them and I laughed heartily at their disconcerted air.

I also saw wonderful birds; macaws, blue and red parrots, and humming birds so tiny and rapid that I took them for brilliant flies. I shot a big cock-of-the-rock which I shall roast this evening. A little farther on, in a marsh edged with high palm trees and bamboos, I saw a big black bird which I recognized as a pelican. The way was made more and more difficult for me by the entanglement of immense ferns, plants with great carved-out leaves,† lianas and lichens which hung from the branches. I recognized, moreover, the scent of trees with precious wood: rosewood, mahogany, and sandalwood. The nearer I came to the source of the river, now a small torrent, the more the trees increased in height and thickness until they met above my head. The branches criss-crossed, hiding the sky, hung with lianas as thick as my arm on which swung the oddest

Shrill-voiced monkeys known as howlers

†Deeply cut leaves: probably philodendrons

Howler monkey

Brown pelican

Breadfruit

Macaw

Agouti

animals in the world, like sloths, a sort of monkey or bear-cub which I only saw hanging by its paws and moving about coolly 30 feet above the ground. Flowers* of a brilliance I had never seen before grew on all the trees. I found also on issuing from the gloomy wood a tree, called Brazil ironwood, which I knew to be very hard, and which I could use to good account.

At midday, I reached the open prairie, the forest having yielded to beautiful clearings of fine grass. Goats† were gambolling there but fled on seeing me. From my first hunting I had seen that I could not approach game except by a trick, the animals here are so agile and timid. Suddenly in a grassy path Japp came to a stop. I saw then some big tawny-coloured furry rodents‡ making off pursued vainly by my dog. Farther off, in a

valley, I discovered a delightful meadow where ran a pretty stream. Tired out, I passed the rest of the afternoon there, overcome by the charm of this place, its peace and freshness. Carpeted by long grass, and shaded by fruit trees of all kinds, it is the ideal place to relax in. I even think of building a cabin there to rest myself and gather fruit. As I do not wish to give up my fortified cave dwelling, I shall make the Valley of Delights my country house.

1 NOVEMBER
I TALK AGAIN OF MY COUNTRY HOUSE

It is a very modest dwelling: a little hut protected by a sloping roof of round logs. Already I have gone there two or three times to rest and eat mangoes and pineapples. I have even

tried the adventure of sleeping there a night or two: I did this three days ago.

Leaving there, after a very good night's sleep, loaded with bread and bananas, accompanied by my dog, I carried the exploration of my island a little farther than the first time. I had walked for half an hour along a valley when I saw in a field of wild sugar-cane a peccary which was grunting as it pushed among the canes. Farther on, I found tobacco plants, which gave me great joy, my supply being nearly exhausted. While moving from valley to plain, I skirted three high hills shaped like sugar-loaves.* I finally arrived in a sort of estuary, which made me think the sea was near, bordered by a strange forest whose trees seemed raised into the air by long aerial roots† which plunged into the mud of a swamp. In the end, after having gone through a big grove of coco-trees, I

stopped short on seeing a magnificent beach. I was evidently on the opposite side from my cave; that is to say, I had crossed the island from side to side, south to north.

On the sand, basking in the sun, crawled numberless turtles. I collected some eggs, much surprised not to have found any of them on the other side of the island; I also picked up some coconuts. I was getting ready to turn back, when, raising my eyes, what was my perplexity to see on the horizon the dark line of a coast I had never seen before. For a moment I believed myself saved! But soon, on second thoughts, fearing that these lands might be inhabited by ferocious cannibals, I no longer dreamed of rescue, and returned soberly to my home.

*Sugarloaf hills:
cones of old volcanoes

†Trees with long aerial roots:
mangroves

*Flowers: orchids, begonias

†Goats probably landed on the island by ships taking on fresh water

‡Rodents with tawny fur: agoutis

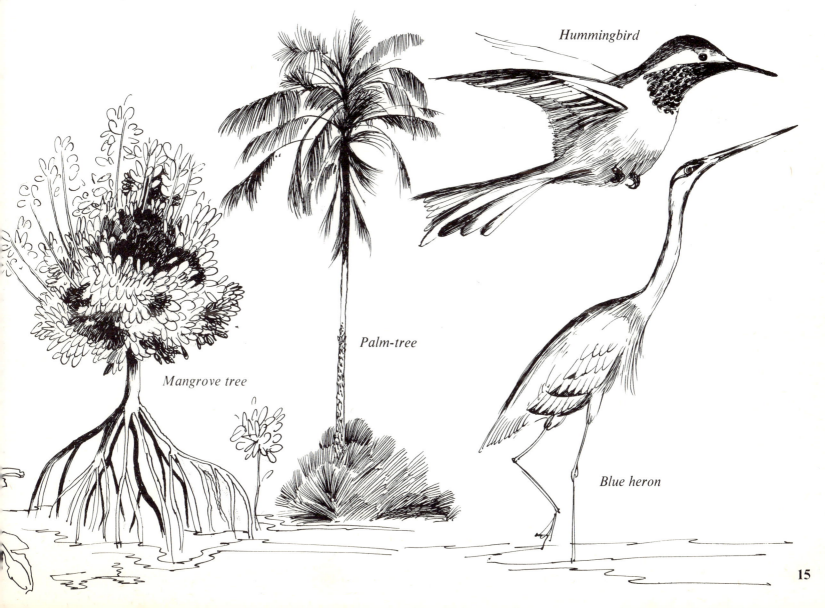

Hummingbird

Mangrove tree

Palm-tree

Blue heron

3 NOVEMBER/I LOSE A DAY'S HUNTING

I had as yet spared nothing, neither powder nor ball, my gun resounded to every echo. But ill-luck relentlessly pursued me. A goat I fired at and wounded rushed away to hide in the undergrowth. I followed it, finding it intolerable both to make the poor beast suffer, and to lose my prey. But at the moment I reached the edge of a fine clump of palm-trees, I fell over a stump, and twisted my knee. Pain paralysed me on the ground for nearly an hour, and the goat profited by this to disappear. I made myself a plaster of leaves which I kept on my knee by tying a stem of rush round it, and, limping badly, I tried to shoot a fat

Pigeon: doubtless passenger pigeons common then and since entirely exterminated by man

†*Hoatzin: crested bird whose young carry to the age of three weeks two claws on their wings (like the archaeopteryx, a prehistoric bird that lived one hundred and fifty million years ago)*

turkey which started up suddenly under my feet. In my haste I missed. I was very glad in the end to bring back a pigeon* and a hoatzin,† a shrill-voiced bird that I could not eat because of its rank-smelling flesh.

I drew nevertheless from this mischance a lesson for the future. What would become of me if I were to be incapacitated from hunting because of illness, or even by lack of powder and shot? I would die of hunger on my wretched bed, at a quarter of a mile from country fuller of game than any I had ever known. I must therefore construct snares and traps.

4 NOVEMBER

Tonight, during a long bout of sleeplessness, my knee being still painful, I made many plans for setting up traps. In the first place, a trap for big game, made of a pit covered with hurdles hidden under grass. I also thought of a smaller trap in which a bird which lights on a baited forked stick makes the support wobble and knocks out of position a stone placed on a slope. The stone falls like a lid, catching the bird, unhurt, at the bottom of a hole. This morning my knee is less swollen and I suffer only a numbness in it. I have made some drawings of traps in my sketchbook.

7 NOVEMBER/FIRST CAPTURE

Two days ago I constructed goat traps. This morning I rushed to visit them. In the first one, nothing. As for the other, melancholy bleatings warned me at once. A big billy-goat was struggling furiously to get out. I felled him at one blow, but, since he was very heavy, I cut him up at the bottom of the pit, and carried home the pieces to roast and dry them.

12 NOVEMBER

This morning I trapped a young wild turkey. Instead of killing him, which would have made me only a paltry dinner, I had the idea of putting him in a cage. His cries and gobblings attracted his mother, who ran round him distractedly. I wished to catch her, but quicker than I, with a flutter of wings she slipped away into the grass.

13 NOVEMBER

I have had to hollow out somewhat deeper the cave which served me as a barn or cellar behind my tent, for the storms have become very violent as the season advances, and my tent canvas is no longer sufficient to protect me from the rain nor my provisions or my property. I plan to set up my home here permanently.

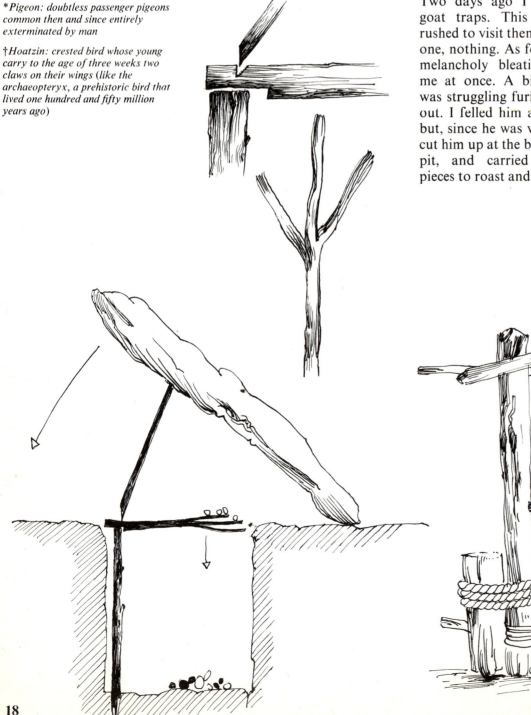

I HAVE GOT MY TURKEY!

I captured her with the help of a box balanced on a small stick tied to a cord which I held. I fastened the young turkey under the box and hid myself behind a bush. At the end of an hour or more, the mother turkey got bolder and came to join her young one. I pulled the cord and the box fell on her. Is this the beginning of a farmyard?

Hunger obliged me to become inventive. I perfected my bird trap, in the sense that I no longer held the cord. I have made a sketch of the apparatus with which I am not too dissatisfied. In one cage a bird trapped by means of the box attracts another bird by his cries. The latter runs up, sees grain scattered on the small board, raids it and trips the stick that holds it down. The cage hanging above falls, imprisoning the second bird. I have trapped in this way two turkeys, four hoccos, and two golden caurales, magnificent birds that I have kept to entertain me.

16 NOVEMBER

I have forgotten to note that I set up my stone bird trap and it has captured successfully a sort of partridge* which flies very badly, like a thrush. I am going to change the apparatus and make the hole bigger. The difficulty will be to find a stone large and flat enough to cover all the opening. I have also laid snares. Yesterday I went to pick them up: what was my surprise to find two agoutis. They would make excellent stews if I had a stewpot.

17 NOVEMBER

I have recaptured my wounded goat! Caught in a trap, one foot broken. Full of pity for so much misery, I cared for her and fed her. She seems not to wish to leave me.

*Partridge: in all probability, a tinamou

Hocco

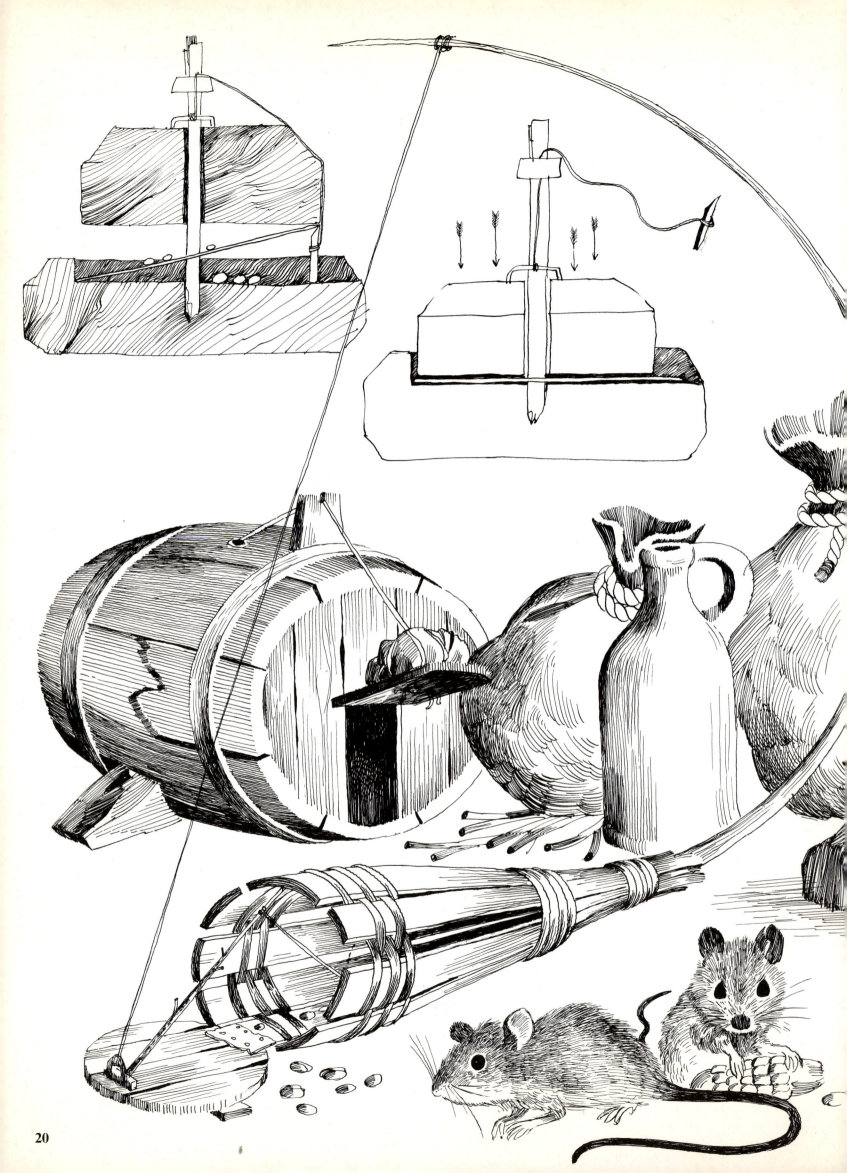

THE FIRST ATTACKERS

On the other hand, certain small animals I could very well do without are mice, rats,* and field-mice, which have infested my pantry for some time. Every morning to my rage I find my bags nibbled, my boxes gnawed, my provisions damaged, and the raiders each day are more insolent and daring. I have tried hard to tame wild-cats, but the brutes make off at the least gesture. What shall I do?

*Rats: rodents landed from ships, and which caused much damage in the Antilles

12 DECEMBER

This morning I found that the small sack of grain, brought from the ship, was half eaten. I shouted with rage and indignation: I hunted the thieves with gunshot, but at the bang bits of the roof of the cave fell off and crashed at my feet. This calmed my exasperation at once.

26 DECEMBER 1659

Yesterday I caught four rats and two fat field-mice with the help of three very fine traps I invented. In the barrel trap, while gnawing a bit of meat which acts as a link between a nail driven into the barrel and a string, they unhook the fastening of a little door weighted with stones. Second, in the funnel trap, the animal slinking off touches the thread stretched across the middle and brings down the slanting twig which wedges the door open. Held tightly by the bow, the door closes like a clapper. As for the fall-trap, the little animal is crushed by the heavy wooden paving-block which falls down when the two upright slanting sticks are knocked over by the intruder.

6 JANUARY 1660

The little grain I have been able to save from the greed of the nibblers, not even enough to make a loaf, was sowed today in a short stretch of ground which I have tilled with a branch. What will become of it?

MY BOWER UNDER THE MANGO TREES

I am writing these lines in the shade of the arbour with which I have adorned my country house. I pass delicious hours here, stretched in a hammock, smoking a pipe, or drawing. Today I feel myself completely happy, and my solitary existence weighs on me lightly when I consider that all the good things nature spreads around me belong to me alone. This morning I picked fruit from my garden, mangoes, pineapples, avocadoes, bananas, guavas, lemons, citrons, grapefruit, melons – I know not what more! My valley is an earthly paradise! I shall try to preserve them by either drying in the sun, or by cooking them in sugar, like jam. I had a rich plantation in Brazil; and I intend to put to profit my planter's experience to extract sugar from the wild canes that grow here in abundance.

One thing I lack unfortunately is big cauldrons, for I have only a pitcher the top of which I have broken off to make a bowl. This will keep down my cooking ambitions.

But patience! My imagination will deal with this problem.

15 FEBRUARY

I am exhausted. Fruit-gathering, a charming pastoral pastime, gives me, alas, a crick in the neck. I have invented to help me in the work the little basket I have sketched below. It is a long pole ending in a four-branched fork, a sort of natural basket the sides of which I have woven with strips of bark. Here is how I use it: I raise the basket, I place it under the desired fruit, and turn it gently, the fruit comes off, and falls softly into the tiny basket. It is perfect. I am thinking also of making a big basket, a sort of grape hamper on a sledge, to fill with fruit to bring it all back in good condition. Here is a sketch of the thing. It is funny-looking. I am not exactly clumsy, but I must confess that it is the first time I have made such an object, and the result is peculiar.

I shall set out tomorrow morning equipped with all my fruit-gathering appliances, before the midday heat. All the same, I must return soon to my castle which I have now been away from for three full days.

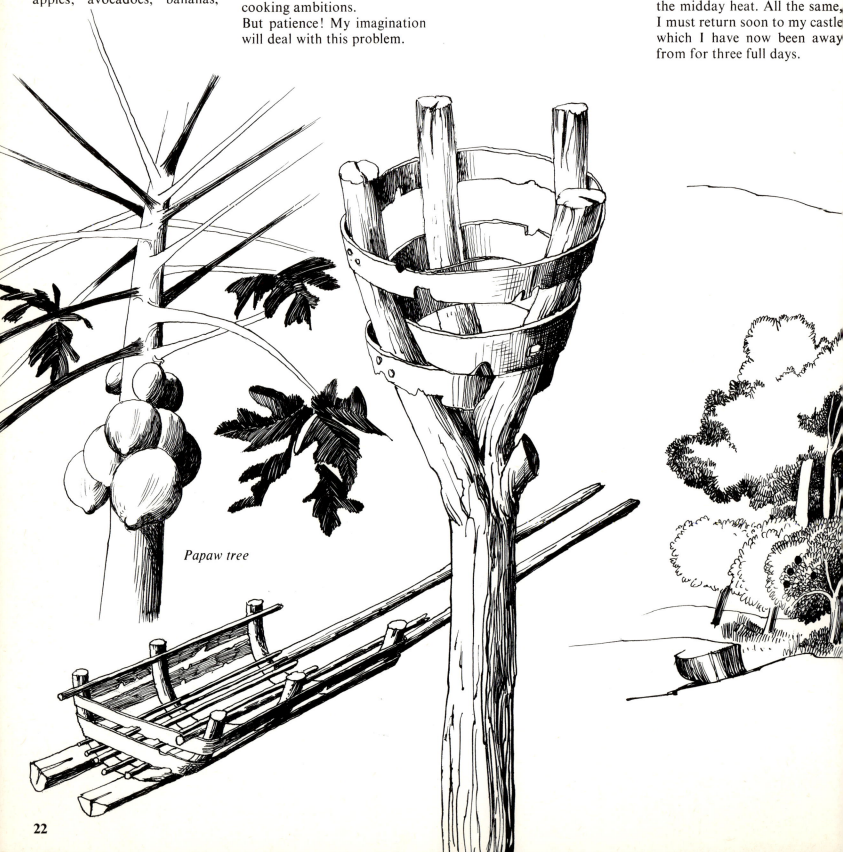

Papaw tree

16 FEBRUARY/ DAMNATION

I have just escaped a terrible danger. My uneasy mind cannot take in that this island so sweet to live in could hold in its depths so many ill elements. Here is what happened. This morning, as planned, I set out from my country house, dragging my sledge-load of fruit, my guns, bags, a young peccary killed in a coffee-grove, a few melons and my dog at my heels.

Suddenly the noise of birds which accompanies all my walks ceased abruptly. Japp, flattened on the ground, hair on end, shivered with terror.

I thought at once that a wild beast was going to spring out. I felt a light quivering under my feet, a herd of bison, at least, I thought. But the rumbling became terrifying, and suddenly I was flung four feet away under a shower of earth and branches, my sledge on top of me, my fruit spilled, my dog howling, as at a death. When I regained my senses, I did not recognize the place where I had been a few seconds before. A deep crevasse opened before me. Whole trees had fallen. Then suddenly the rumbling of the ground began again. I understood at last what had happened: it was an earthquake. The island is going to be swallowed up by a tidal wave, I thought in horror. Three times the ground trembled. When, at the end of an hour, the birds began timidly

to sing again, I got up at last, dusted off my clothes, picked up my fruit, three-parts spoiled by the fall, and resumed my journey, racked by a horrid foreboding.

Arriving at my cave, I saw at once that if I had been there at the moment of the cataclysm I would have been killed. My tent was crushed under rocks. The entrance was closed by a landslide. I had to pull out rubble for two hours before I

was able to enter. The roof of the cave had fallen in two places, at the back and at the entrance. All my piled-up goods were buried in over two feet of earth, dust, and pebbles. Until a late hour of the day on which I note these events, I worked to put everything back as before. But there will be plenty of time for that.

I strengthened the roof as well as I could with small beams. I set up my tent, but I could not eat. I am now trying to sleep, sad at heart, and much tormented by the urgent question: ought I not to do everything possible to get away from this island?

MUST I LEAVE MY ISLAND?

I must tear myself away from my island whose charms are so treacherous. The memory of the unknown coast seen twenty leagues away remains with me. Why should I not land there with the help of a small boat which I could make myself? I run a great risk of perishing in this mad enterprise, but to remain for my whole life eating my heart out in loneliness on this island, is that any better? What shall I do?

21 FEBRUARY

I have decided. I am building a dug-out boat. Yesterday I picked out a fine oak-tree trunk, and I have started to cut it down with a hatchet. It is hard work. I have caught a kid in the trap and roasted it.

24 FEBRUARY

A rainstorm yesterday afternoon. My work goes on under the showers. I do not stop, my great desire to escape from my prison sustains me. This morning I cut down the tree, and I have begun lopping off the branches: the work will take me three days. I hope to roll the trunk by means of levers and round logs as far as the creek where I first landed, which is low-lying and well sheltered. The sea is less than 40 feet from there.

A CANOE UNLIKE ANY OTHER

From dawn to sunset I work on, only stopping to visit my traps. The dug-out is in fine trim: to be more modest, I should say only that it looks like a strong canoe. But what labour! Today I put a bad notch in a good carpenter's hatchet: happily I brought back from the wreck a grindstone which will put it right again.

18 APRIL

Yesterday I had the idea of hollowing out my boat by means of fire. I had begun to carve out the more delicate parts with mallet and chisel, but I despaired of the length and difficulty of the work. I made on the ground close by a well-stoked fire, then I placed heaps of embers on the knots and hardest places. The wood burned with heavy smoke, for it was green, but I watched its burning carefully, and stopped it in time by scattering the embers. I think this process is not new, and must have been used by natives before me.

This morning I trapped a fine turkey. My trap works excellently now that I have weighted the falling cage with small stones.

25 MAY 1660
I LEAVE MY ISLAND

I spent some hours this afternoon in sketching my boat. I should explain that yesterday I made such an effort to raise my mast, not having taken time to rope it, that I almost broke my back. What shall I say of my canoe? I find her very handsome and very comfortable. As I had no anchor I thought that a wooden one would do. I devised, I think, a very pretty anchor, of wood and stone fastened together, which is on the lower left of my drawing. I intend to go to sea on first or second June, for the tides being less then, I hope to avoid the risk of being thrown on the rocks, or run aground on the shoals.

2 JUNE

The die is cast. It is time for me to leave this island where for almost a year I believed I could live peacefully; but events have taught me, alas, that I must escape from it. I jot down these last few words in my journal which I have brought with me as well as my sketchbooks, carefully rolled up in a tarpaulin. It is five or six in the morning, I have put Japp on board: the tide is favourable, the winds are gentle. May God protect me!

4 JUNE

Alas! In spite of all the care I had taken to get ready to escape by sea, here I am returned to the fold: disappointed and still shaken by the risks I have run.

Here is what happened: I set off at six o'clock on second June from the little creek where I had launched my canoe. She handled very stylishly, though with a slight list to port. I placed my ballast accordingly, raised my sail, and the gentle breeze at once carried me away from the shore and along the rocky coast on which our vessel had been wrecked. I was just sadly saluting the place of our shipwreck when, suddenly, between two rocks, I saw some flotsam, a barrel and planks. I wanted to look at them closer, but my canoe, now not very manageable, instead of responding to my manoeuvre, began to pitch and roll, not far from a reef where black rocks cropped out dangerously. I had to lower my sail and free myself from the eddy with an oar before I could regain the open sea. I resolved to avoid the rocks, and I made a big detour to round the point west of the island. But the wind dropped, and I began to float round and round like a cork. I rowed strongly towards the coast and at the end of an hour I came to land near a kind of marshy place, planted with those trees with curious roots which had already interested me.* Not far away, on a small hill, I made a fire to cook my dinner and drive away the mosquitoes. I despaired at not being able to leave the island, for I saw, very far away it is true, the coast of the continent or island which had given me that dream of liberty three or four months before. For three hours I hesitated while around me pink ibises and green herons splashed in the mud, and a little farther off, where the marsh had dried up, salt crystals shone like precious

Mangroves

stones. Then, a gust of wind having risen, I boldly launched my canoe and set off again.

I rounded the north west point, and at once my boat was snatched by a strong current which showed against the surrounding sea by its darker water. I realized very quickly that neither my sail nor my oars or rudder would be much use, and I was horrified when I saw that this current, dividing into two distinct streams, was rushing towards the reefs a mile away. I did not dare imagine my fate when my helpless canoe reached the reefs which reared up among violent whirlpools of foam. My sail hung completely limp along the mast. I was powerless against this blow of fate, and the more despairing at the thought that my foolish obstinacy alone had led me to this terrifying extremity. My canoe spun along at a great rate, quicker and quicker, and I wrung my hands. But suddenly I felt on my face a fresh breath of wind, followed by a little gust which swelled my sail, making it flap hopefully. At once I tacked, trying to take advantage of the wind, and little by little, fighting with all my strength, I succeeded in dragging my canoe away from the fearful pull of the current. I was able to turn back towards the island, profiting by the strengthening west wind to round the northern point of the island where I was very quickly in shelter. But when I thought I would come to shore in a quiet cove reflecting the coconut palms, my boat struck violently on a sunken reef. I veered into deeper water, very worried at not having seen anything, when I struck again so heavily that the bow reared up, and I almost fell into the water. I struck again in the stern. Unable to retrieve my balance I dropped into the bottom of my canoe which began to turn round and round. In the height of my puzzlement I was beginning to believe in demons and sorcery, when I saw springing from the water a huge dolphin, who plunged and disappeared. He had caused my confusion. But now at last I could come to shore and pull my boat up on the sand.

I rested there for a few minutes to recover myself, before finally swearing that I would never more attempt to go to sea.

Was I a prisoner on the island? Very well, so be it! I accept my fate. I was so shaken by these dramatic turns of fortune that I even gave up continuing to explore the eastern circuit of the island, not knowing at all what currents, reefs, sea monsters and other dangers awaited me on those shores. I hid my canoe under a grove of coconut palms, and, only taking the essentials, I whistled up my dog and returned to my home, very happy to tread the soil of my kingdom, which seemed to me, in spite of its earthquakes, a hundred times safer than the abysses of the sea.

6 JUNE
COURAGE!

I got up this morning with despair in my heart. My sea adventure left me no longer any hope of flight. I felt a bitter sense of defeat and disappointment, but also a deep thankfulness to Providence for bringing me back safe and sound on the good earth without making me suffer any injury except that of fear, which no one dies of. I must nevertheless do my utmost to improve my condition on the island instead of living like a savage, ill-nourished, and with eyes always fixed upon the sea.

7 JUNE

Since yesterday renewed courage sustains me. I am inspired with ideas for making tools and objects which I have missed terribly up to now. First of all, baskets; for I must confess that, apart from a sort of sledge which I drag to bring back fruit or turtles' eggs or haunches of goat, I have never attempted what can be done in basket-making.

15 JUNE

I have already noted that in the course of my walks on the island I have discovered a plant for which I would give up almost all the forest flowers, however splendid; I mean tobacco plants. I have already grown some and dried the leaves to fill my pipe, for my supply of tobacco brought from the ship has run out. I have also discovered, opportunely enough, stems of a very supple osier as well as liana fibres which when reft of their bark and split longways become the very thing for basket-making. I shall also use tree-bark cut into long thongs, soaked, washed, scraped, and dried in the shade so that they keep their flexibility. I shall start this work tomorrow morning.

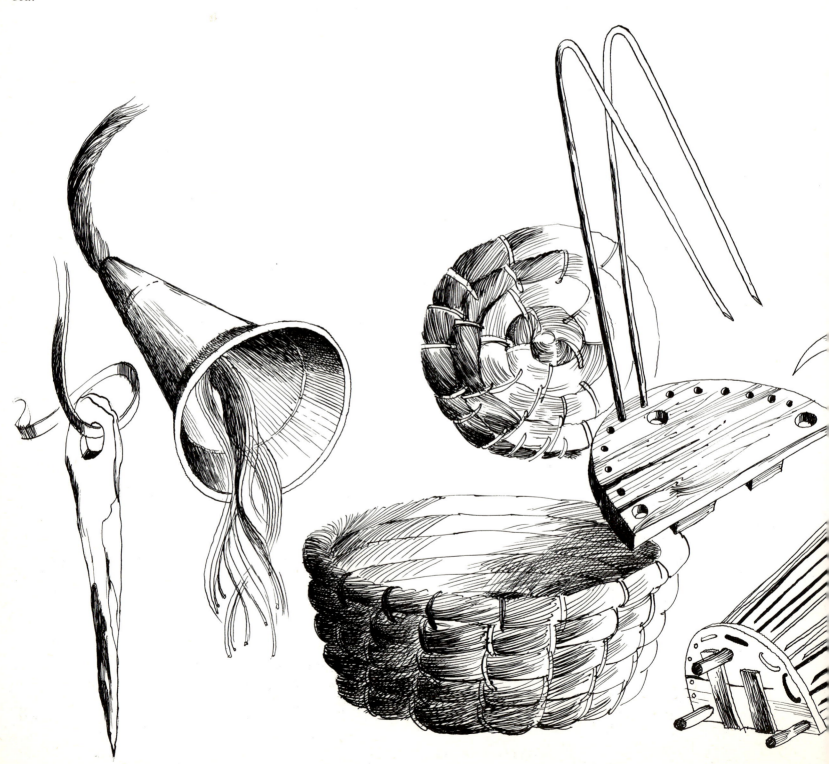

20 JUNE/MY FIRST ATTEMPTS AT BASKET-MAKING

I have succeeded in making a deep basket, very handy and light, which I carry on my back. The base is made of a barrel base halved, the sides of flexible canes are interlaced with strips of bark. I have not yet tried to make osier baskets; but I have had an idea, arising from the barley straw which grows in abundance here, of making a kind of large cup, or bowl, out of sausages of twisted straw which I place spirally on top of each other, sewing them together with thin bramble bark. So that my straw twists may always be of the same thickness, I have made use of the captain's speaking-trumpet. I put into the bell of the trumpet a handful of straw fibre which I draw out to the end of this improvised funnel. Then I twist it lightly, coil it, and sew it. For all its strangeness, this bowl garnished with fruit looks very well.

JUNE 1660/I SET UP MY BASKET WORKSHOP

Little rain these days. A dry heat brings thirst to man, beasts and plants. In the rainy season the river crossing is difficult, even dangerous, for the current is swift and the ebb and flow of the tide makes the eddy more violent. But at this time, in the dry season, the river-level being lower, great stones stand up from the bottom of the stream, and these allow me to cross easily to search for lianas and other materials in the forest.

Certainly I must present a very odd appearance to any observer who should catch me returning from my collecting, as, all wound round with rolls of bark and lianas, dragging rods and long stems behind me,

I jump from rock to rock, at risk a hundred times of falling into the water.

I have made a habit of setting down my bundle of fibres on the river-side, in the hollow of a sort of little natural basin of water, formed by a half-circle of big stones. I preserve this carefully, for the work with osier requires water to clean and soften the canes before weaving the baskets. It would not be any use if the water were to leak out between two stones.

There, under a big bushy mango-tree, I have set up my basket workshop. I have placed in a box a small knife, a pruning-knife to cut the canes, a bodkin to push through the uprights, and a little mallet. I set to work with a touching zeal, for in spite of my efforts,

and my childhood memories (we had a basket-maker as a neighbour whom I loved to watch working) I have not up to now succeeded in weaving anything but shapeless flat baskets.

HOW I MAKE A BASKET

This morning a growling of thunder announcing a storm surprised me in the middle of my work. Everything breathes rain and freshness now. I have done well to persevere in basket-making, for after many miserable attempts which made me laugh I have at last got a basket to sit properly, by beginning the bottom with a cross-piece, as my good friend the basket-maker used to do. Here is how I do it: I cut eight uprights of osier as long as the width of my basket, $1\frac{1}{2}$ feet. I slit four of them in the middle to slip in four others, which makes a cross. I take a long well-damped liana and place it astride one of the arms of the

cross, the north arm, for instance. I have then a stem that hangs to the left and another to the right. I cross the two stems and get them to pass one over and one under the east arm of the cross; then I cross them again and pass them respectively above and below the south arm, and so on for three turns. After that, I divide each arm of the cross in two, which gives me eight arms which I fasten in the same way as before for two turns. Then I separate again into two each of the eight arms of the cross, which gives me sixteen arms, spreading them out like the spokes of a wheel, well fastened by the crossed stems of the same liana. Now I thrust between two of the arms an extra arm, in order to get an unequal number of spokes. I then take a cane of

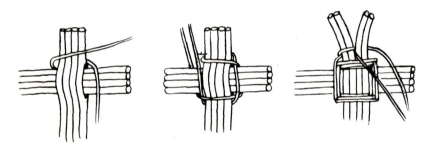

Extra upright →

In these two drawings Robinson wished to make plain that you can avoid the stage of separating the uprights into eight arms by dividing them at once into sixteen arms ▼

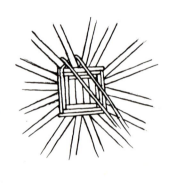

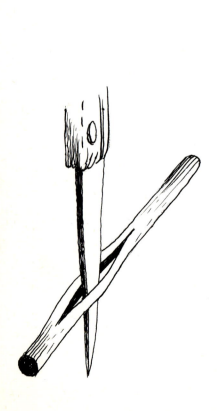

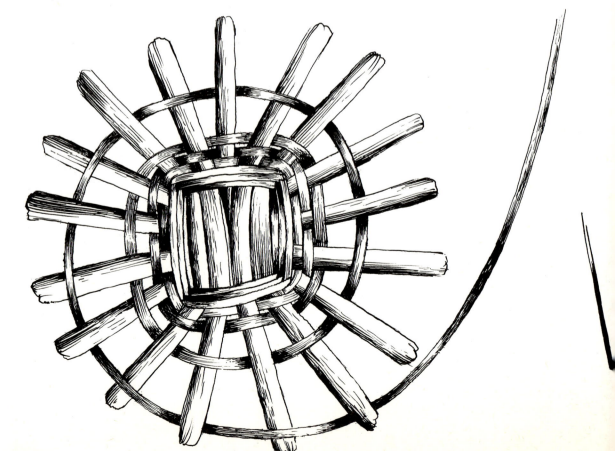

osier which I push in near an arm. I pass it over this arm, then under the next arm, then over the next, and so on. Thus I roll my willow cane spirally while pressing strongly down on the weaving. If the willow cane is not long enough, I take another cane which I fasten to the place where the first one finishes, taking care to let the ends go inside the basket, and I continue my weaving. When the base is finished I push in the end of the osier cane along one arm, and I cut the seventeen arms level with the weaving. Then, to make the sides, I thrust long canes very deeply into each side of each arm, and then bend them up straight again, doubling them over first to fold them. Now I have thirty-four vertical uprights. To strengthen the base of the basket I weave a sort of twisted cord or braid made with three canes. Now, with one stem of liana as for the base, I interweave the body of the basket. It is still necessary to leave the uprights free for the length of three full hands to make the border. I turn in the uprights after having cut them neatly on the slant and I push them into the woven part. I have a choice between two borders, whether I push each riser along the next one, or whether I miss one, thus getting interlaced arches. By leaving two higher arches

than the others, diametrically opposite and very strongly bound, I make handles.

Thus I have constructed round baskets, long ones, high ones, small ones, game baskets, grain hampers, in which I store my fruit, my food, and all kinds of provisions, protected from the dust and damp of my cave.

Making a "twist" or braid of three canes:
Take three long canes of osier and insert them near three uprights. The first cane passes before two uprights, then behind the next, returns to the front and remains waiting. Do the same with the second and third canes and continue for two or three rounds. A border can be made with only one round

Making a handle:
One of the uprights has been raised and curved along another upright, and then they have been strongly fastened and bound to the top of the border

Hamper: big grain basket

12 JULY 1660/CORN!

If one of my tame golden caurales had not escaped recently, I would not have had the lucky idea of pursuing it under the trees as far as the small field where I had sowed my few poor grains of corn some months earlier. Japp had succeeded in catching the bird by the tail, and I was going to pick up the fugitive, when I saw vaguely that the soil trampled on by the two silly young creatures was marked with points of tall gilt shoots: corn! I fell on my knees, more to thank Heaven for its infinite bounty than to count the few stems. There were full thirty or forty of them, and I promised myself to harvest them when ripe and to sow them again in the hope of one day being able to make bread. As for my escaped bird, I found him again pecking at my green lawn and strutting about with loud clappings of his beak as if nothing had happened.

2 SEPTEMBER
I TRY MY HAND AT POTTERY

Truth to tell, I had to train myself to make pottery because cooking utensils, pots and pitchers, were all wanting. Having discovered in a valley behind my hill a bed of superb red clay, I decided to try my hand at this craft, for which as yet I had no inclination. I learnt to my cost that the clay should be long and strongly kneaded to get rid of pebbles and impurities. By treading it with bare feet, like a wine-maker treading grapes, I succeeded in getting a good smooth paste without air bubbles.

To make a pot, I shape a sort of clay cake, very flat and round, then, taking balls of paste, I roll them with my hand on a damp slab to make sausages which I roll up in more or less bell-shaped circles so as to form the sides of the pot. I then leave my pots to dry first of all in the shade, then in the sun, smoothing out the bulges with the well-wetted palm of my hand. I am always surprised by the ugliness and clumsiness of my work.

30 SEPTEMBER 1660

Yesterday I picked up a ball of clay that had fallen into the fire I had hastily made to roast a turkey. I found that the baked earth was perfectly smooth and hard, like metal, at least almost so! At once, I placed the dried pots one on top of the other and carefully piled bundles of wood all round them. I placed stones to crown the dome-shaped heap, smaller and smaller ones right to the top, and then I set fire to the furnace. It was about nightfall. Time to eat a scrap, smoke a pipe lit with a brand from the furnace, and then my kiln was lit up like a lantern. All night long I looked after my fire. I could have read a verse from the Bible at its fine ruddy light. It was only at dawn this morning that I let the fire die down. And then, as with great impatience I demolished the heap of stones, the thought came to me that it was the thirtieth September 1660, the anniversary of my landing on the island.

Uncovering beside my extinct kiln, I rendered thanks to the Lord for having saved me a year ago precisely. As joy seldom comes alone, I then discovered in the ashes three bowls, two pitchers, and a cooking-pot, fearsomely ugly, but hard and perfectly watertight. As soon as it was cold again, I put my pot on the fire with water, a piece of meat, salt, sweet potatoes, and beans. I let the whole simmer, and at midday I had the joy of tasting the finest stew of my life.

I BECOME AN EXPERIENCED POTTER

My earthenware was so rough and so thick that in spite of the success of my first attempt, I still had trouble in obtaining faultless pots. So I had the idea of constructing a wheel. Very simple and very rustic, but very effective. I made a big wheel, at the cost of much effort, whose axle turned in the socket of an ironwood base. Above this wheel I placed a bench, on which I sat. One of my feet rested on a bar of wood, the other foot by little kicks kept the wheel continually moving. All I had to do then was to place a ball of worked clay on the wheel-hub, then with my hands pressing or slackening I formed the pot. I push my fist gently forward, I hollow out, the belly curves, the wall becomes thinner, the object rises. With my wetted hands I polish the surface, and I finish my pot by narrowing the neck. With the help of a wire I detach the base from the hub, and set my pot to dry before being baked. But what horrors I have been the author of, before making objects a little more creditable! Shapeless jugs, huge pots, collapsing flasks, twisted bowls! I have kept as a souvenir a horrible bowl from which Japp, a good eater, and not caring anything for beauty, laps his soup without raising an eyebrow.

NOVEMBER 1661
I BECOME A MASTER SMITH

I am black from head to foot, because I have just come back from my wood, where I have spent two days making charcoal. I should have said, first of all, that I badly need wood charcoal to feed my kiln. For I bake my bread in it (I have had two fine harvests of corn this year), I harden my pottery in it, and I bring to a red heat in it the metal I use to forge my tools. All these crafts demand a good steady and lively furnace.

I must confess that it is now, at the end of two years of mistakes and disappointments, that I really begin to live better. Thanks in the first place to this oven I have built in stone. Below is the hearth where I blow the flames and embers to a very high temperature. Above, I arrange bread, earthenware, or even haunches of goat. Gaps arranged between the stones separating the two layers allow the heat to pass through. An earthenware pipe serves as chimney. I close my oven with an iron door, a solid cover taken from a sea-chest, stoutly fastened with clasps. When I want to forge the tools I make with the iron I have salvaged from the ship's hull, I place the furnace in the upper part; and to get a more intense blaze, as the iron must redden to white heat, I set a bellows going. My anvil is a huge axe driven into a stump, well lashed and tied so that it does not split.

A MASTER CHARCOAL-BURNER!

The furnace would not have given me all this satisfaction if I had not had the idea of feeding it with charcoal. To make this precious fuel I build a sort of chimney made of big logs placed upright and ringed with a heap of small round logs

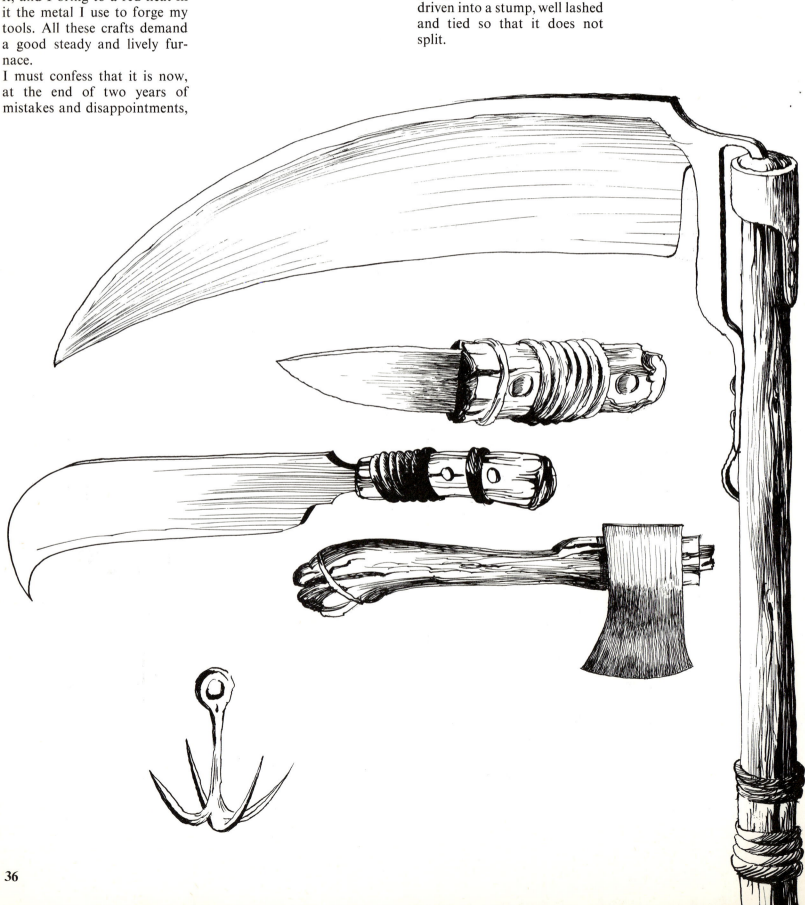

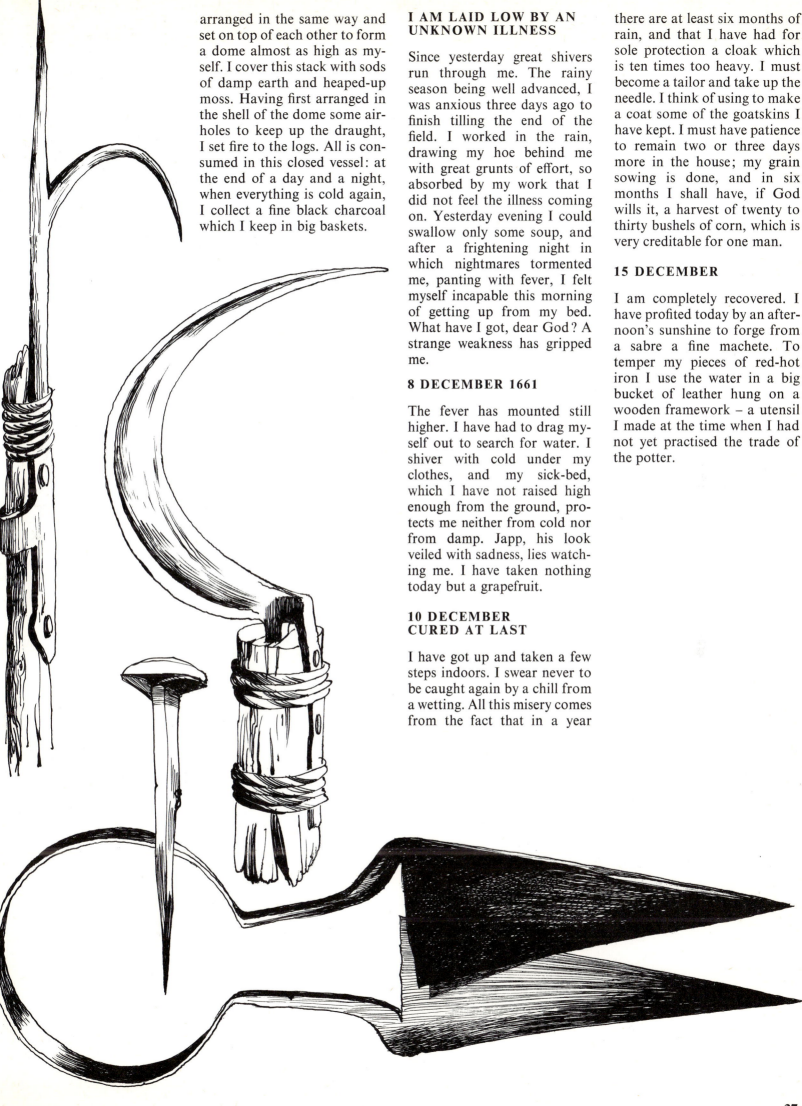

arranged in the same way and set on top of each other to form a dome almost as high as myself. I cover this stack with sods of damp earth and heaped-up moss. Having first arranged in the shell of the dome some air-holes to keep up the draught, I set fire to the logs. All is consumed in this closed vessel: at the end of a day and a night, when everything is cold again, I collect a fine black charcoal which I keep in big baskets.

I AM LAID LOW BY AN UNKNOWN ILLNESS

Since yesterday great shivers run through me. The rainy season being well advanced, I was anxious three days ago to finish tilling the end of the field. I worked in the rain, drawing my hoe behind me with great grunts of effort, so absorbed by my work that I did not feel the illness coming on. Yesterday evening I could swallow only some soup, and after a frightening night in which nightmares tormented me, panting with fever, I felt myself incapable this morning of getting up from my bed. What have I got, dear God? A strange weakness has gripped me.

8 DECEMBER 1661

The fever has mounted still higher. I have had to drag myself out to search for water. I shiver with cold under my clothes, and my sick-bed, which I have not raised high enough from the ground, protects me neither from cold nor from damp. Japp, his look veiled with sadness, lies watching me. I have taken nothing today but a grapefruit.

10 DECEMBER CURED AT LAST

I have got up and taken a few steps indoors. I swear never to be caught again by a chill from a wetting. All this misery comes from the fact that in a year there are at least six months of rain, and that I have had for sole protection a cloak which is ten times too heavy. I must become a tailor and take up the needle. I think of using to make a coat some of the goatskins I have kept. I must have patience to remain two or three days more in the house; my grain sowing is done, and in six months I shall have, if God wills it, a harvest of twenty to thirty bushels of corn, which is very creditable for one man.

15 DECEMBER

I am completely recovered. I have profited today by an afternoon's sunshine to forge from a sabre a fine machete. To temper my pieces of red-hot iron I use the water in a big bucket of leather hung on a wooden framework – a utensil I made at the time when I had not yet practised the trade of the potter.

30 SEPTEMBER 1662
THIRD ANNIVERSARY OF MY ARRIVAL IN THE ISLAND

This morning I recollected myself for some minutes, to commemorate the day of my landing on this island. When I think of the horrible circumstances of my shipwreck, of my distress of mind when I was saved, of the first hours I passed on the island in the most absolute destitution, I can only contrast those terrible memories with my present condition and thank Heaven for my well-being, enjoying good things, sheltered from the turmoil of the inhabited world, and unrivalled master of a marvellous kingdom. In sign of gratitude I planted on the hill facing the sea a young gumdragon tree,* which Japp saluted with joyful barking. In all these festivities I do not forget for long to draw on the slighter resources of my island. Thus, this afternoon about six o'clock I went fishing where, luck aiding me, I caught in less than half an hour three mackerel and four beautiful scarlet fish.†

*Gumdragon:
tree giving blood-red gum when cut

†Scarlet fish:
probably red beryx or coral fish

3 OCTOBER
MY FISHERY

Without wishing to boast, I have become quite a good fisherman, from the day when having observed that, in the ebb and flow of the tide, shoals of big and small fish were swimming near the mouth of the river, I had the idea of building a covered raft raised on a

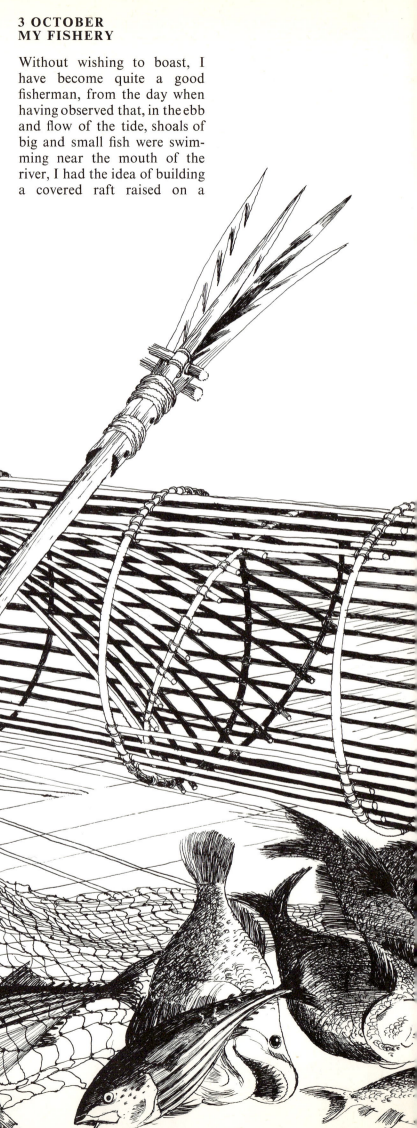

sandbank which stood across the entrance to the inlet. Afterwards I stored there my nets, baskets, lines, harpoons, and other fishing gear which I have been able to plan and make during these past months. I can very easily hang nets across the stream, and fish in the current without danger. Since my poor beautiful canoe is rotting under the trees in the end of a creek, for want of being able to drag

her near my house, I have had to build a second boat, much smaller, to make my journeys to and fro between the covered raft and the bank.

I have given up making boats in wood, which cost me too much time and effort. I have simply stretched goatskins over a solid framework of osier. This small boat is a bit tricky to manage, but the fault is made up for by its lightness and the ease with which I can lift it up on the raft or on the shore. Instead of an anchor, I have caged a large stone in a net I have woven. My hooks are curved nails shaped with a hammer: I have a great number of hooks of different sizes. There is nothing that I have not done with my own hands, for I brought back from the ship as fishing gear only a coil of rope and one of rope-yarn.

12 NOVEMBER 1662
MARVELLOUS FISHING

Overcast weather. Fine rain, but I have decided in spite of it to try fishing. Well for me that I did so! I have caught the finest fish I have ever seen out of water, a sword-fish! As well as two or three tunny-fish, a small shark, some flying-fish and a moon-fish. I have enough to feed me, taking care to preserve the flesh in salt, for at least a month or more.

AUGUST 1663/MY CABINS IN THE TREES

At the time of my sea voyage; I should write "my ordeal", for the memory of those terrifying hours has not left me; I noticed some tall trees on the coast, and the idea of climbing them to command the horizon attracted me, in case a ship bent her sails towards me, and also to survey my island and its surroundings. I built therefore, at the four corners of the island, little hanging tree-platforms from which I amused myself by observing the magnificent birds that surrounded me: toucans, macaws, parakeets. Climbing these trees is not easy: I climb with a rope-ladder, but when I am old it will no longer be possible to think of it. I sometimes have visitors, little monkeys who come to steal my bread, my inkpots, and my pens, for I sketch a little everywhere. So I have had to hang canvas round to close off my cabins when I leave them. I have captured a young parrot and taught him to say his name, Poll, and mine. He and I have long absurd conversations.

JULY 1664
WAR AGAINST FEATHERED THIEVES

I am furious! My corn is almost ripe: I should be beginning to sharpen my reaping-hooks and scythes to cut it eight days from now. But, alas, a month ago hundreds of birds pounced on my field and pillaged it without mercy. Three times a day now I fire musket shots to frighten away the robbers. Flocks of birds rise screeching, and as soon as my back is turned throw themselves again on my poor harvest. I have an idea . . .

4 JULY

Here is what I have devised. But first let me tell you that three years ago, if I mistake not, I made some clothes in goatskin to protect me from the rain. A very bad chill had much weakened me at the period of the year 1661, when rain and storms had changed my island into a slough. These clothes, made in haste, badly cut and badly sewn, had never pleased me. I had worn them for two years, then put them away in the bottom of a chest when I had made a second suit from suppler skins. This latter, better fitting, was composed of a jacket, breeches, and a cap. To make the rain slip off easily, I had taken care to put the fur on the outside. I had also made a goatskin umbrella to shelter me both from the rain and from the heat of the sun. I succeeded moreover in jointing the umbrella so as to fold it; the first one, of clumsier make, would not close. This morning then, I have had a notion to stuff with straw my old clothes and to erect them on sticks to make an effigy. I have planted this scarecrow in the middle of the field, cap on head, protected by the old umbrella and armed with fearsome wooden guns and pistols. The resemblance is perfect. Henceforth, day and night, a Robinson Crusoe on sentry-go who watches for marauders!

Harrow

Plough

Flail

WHAT LABOUR TO MAKE BREAD!

I have had to dig, sow, harrow, roll, cut, harvest, beat, thresh, grind, and sift my flour, and to make a huge number of tools and objects to assist me. Very luckily I had been able to recover at low tide the last shipment from the wreck, which was engulfed when my raft capsized five years ago. A load of iron salvaged from the hull, chains, and ironwork from the rudder which I have converted into a ploughshare and a scythe. It pleases me to think that this iron, after having ploughed the sea, now breaks deep furrows in the fostering earth. I have also had to provide a mortar which I carved in a log of ironwood, and rolled right into my kitchen, as well as a pestle of the same wood. I have woven a winnowing basket but it will take two years for me to find the perfect shape. As for the sieve, I made it with a solid thong of bark rolled into a circle on which I have hung one of the last fine shirts found in the captain's sea-chest.

VICTORY!

The frightened robber birds have deserted my field! There are indeed some bolder ones who still flutter about and come to pounce on a field of beans which I cultivated 20 feet away, and whose paling does nothing to prevent the robbery. I have surrounded my pasture with a fence made of the willow wood which I used for the hedge of my dwelling, and I should note down the curious thing about this: the stakes driven into the ground have taken root, and are almost budding. I am happy about this for I shall soon have a leafy grove around my dwellings.

This paling budded as did the earlier ones; I have now very pretty living hedges on my land, and I know why my calendar post has not sprouted; I planted it head downwards, the sap is the wrong way round and cannot make the stem put out roots. I have some posts in my hedges also which refuse to sprout.

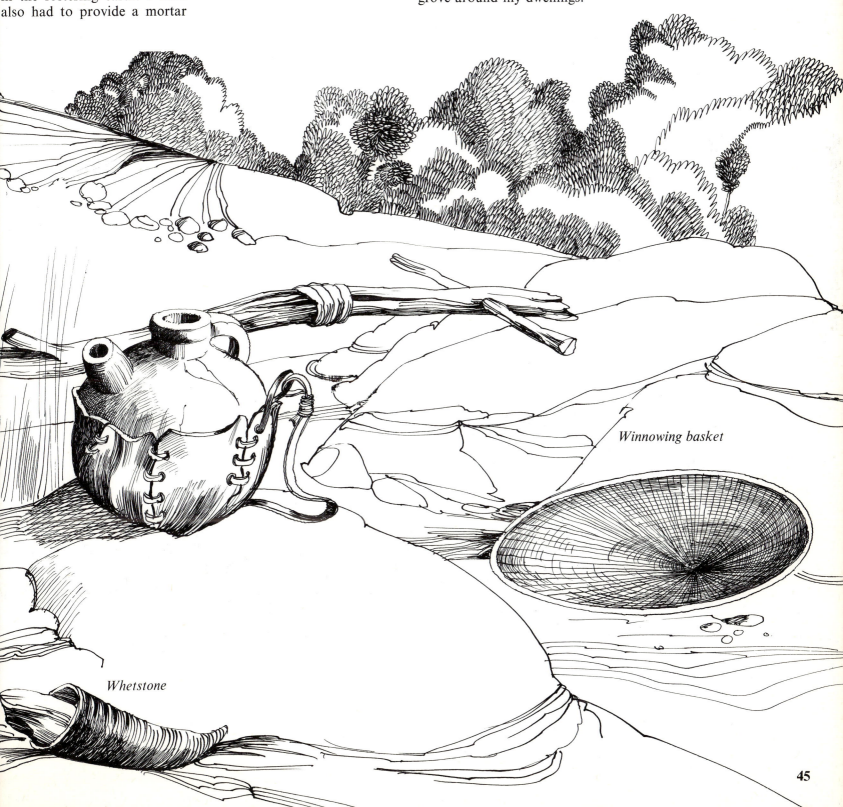

Winnowing basket

Whetstone

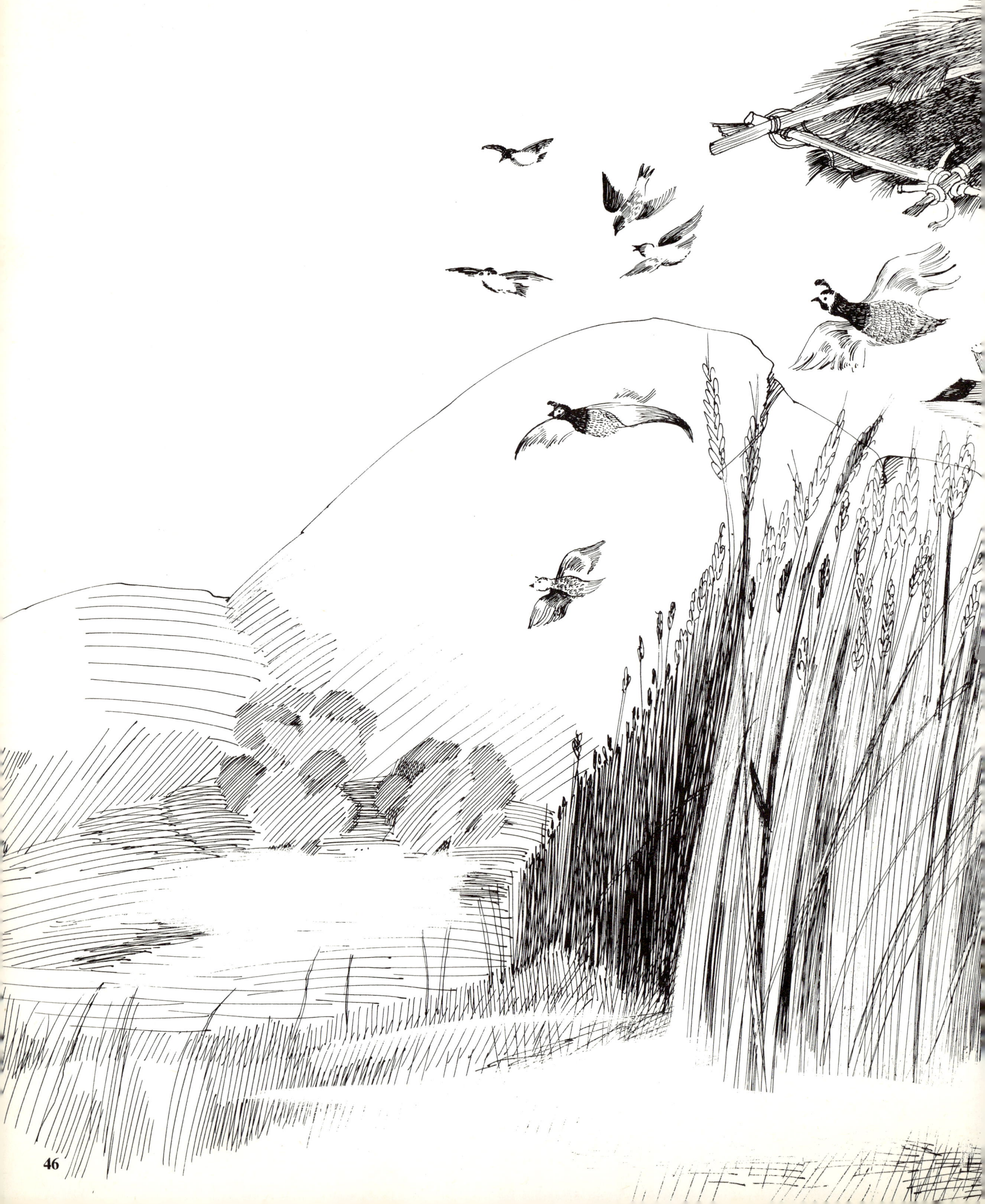

MARCH 1667
A VERY FINE HERD

I came on a charming scene today at the bottom of one of my traps. A goat which had fallen in with its kid, was quietly giving it milk without worrying apparently at seeing nothing but a tiny corner of sky above its horns. I have already captured three mothers and their little ones, and far from separating them, I tend them carefully in an enclosure in a meadow by the river, at some distance from my home. If I happen to lack meat I shall be provided at once. Furthermore, I have milk. Nevertheless my dairy-farm worries me; even though it is situated near a stream, I have great difficulty in raising enough water for my herd to drink. Twice a day I have to lower nine or ten heavy jars at the end of a rope, and bring them up again full, by the strength of my arm.

My herd of goats comprises twenty-three head, of which three are he-goats. This farm of livestock gives me plenty of work certainly, but I should be wrong to complain of it; for if I milk, clean, spread hay and

straw, fill up the drinking-trough, and sometimes run the risk of receiving a good butting, I have the satisfaction of drinking fresh milk, of making butter and cheese, of always having meat, fat for my candles, and superb goatskins. These I hang in the sun, after having scraped them and rubbed them with salt to preserve them.

My main difficulty, as I have already said, was to raise the water to the drinking-trough. But a few days ago I had the idea of making my rope pass over a pulley, and of replacing my jars by a big and much lighter goatskin bag. Yesterday I set the operation going, and I must say the result encouraged me to look even further. Why should I not make a water-mill, using a little waterfall which murmurs away at a stone's throw from my pasture? I would be able to grind my corn

there instead of pounding it in a mortar, as I have always done. I was emboldened even to think of constructing a wind-mill, for clearly there is not a waterfall on the island which has enough power to drive a big wheel . . . but I stray from

the subject. To construct such a machine is not an easy matter and there are other things just now which concern me. I mean my weapons, for, if I do not take care, and continue to hunt in the forest, in spite of my snares, traps, and my herd, I shall soon have no more powder.

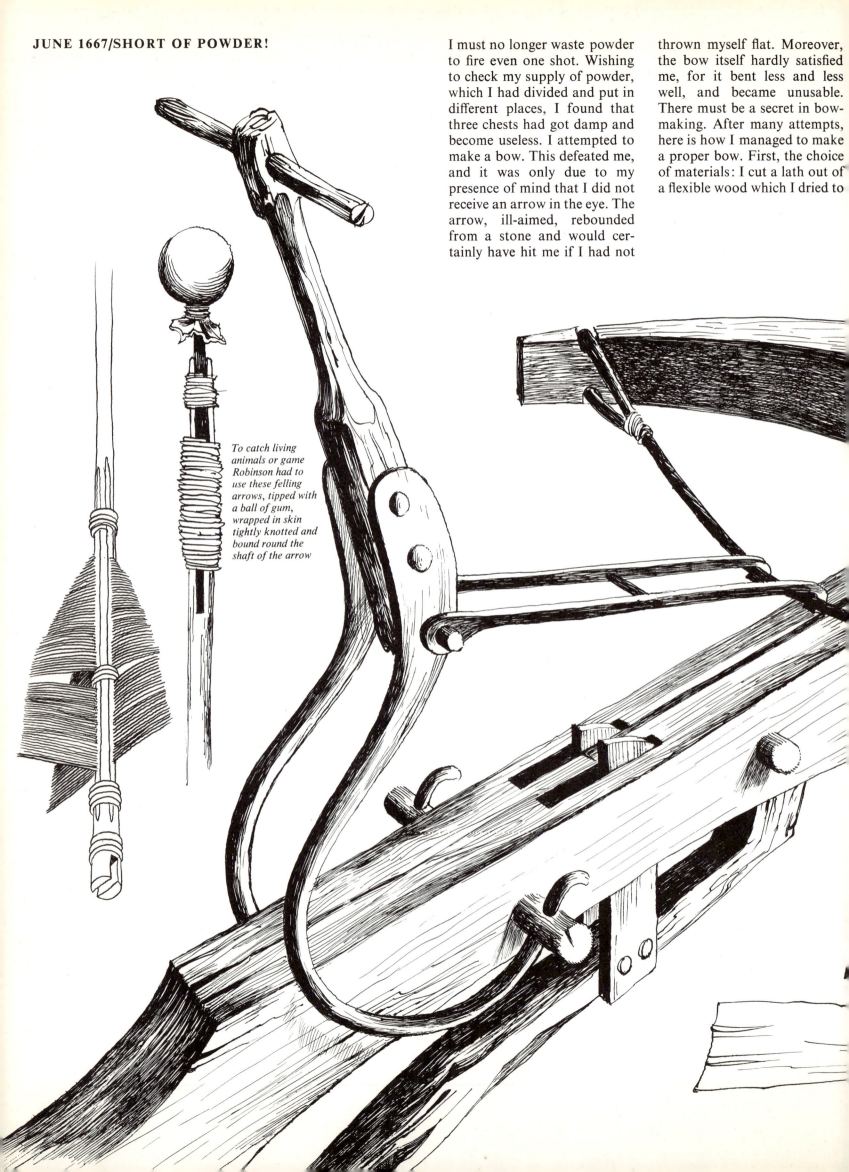

To catch living animals or game Robinson had to use these felling arrows, tipped with a ball of gum, wrapped in skin tightly knotted and bound round the shaft of the arrow

I must no longer waste powder to fire even one shot. Wishing to check my supply of powder, which I had divided and put in different places, I found that three chests had got damp and become useless. I attempted to make a bow. This defeated me, and it was only due to my presence of mind that I did not receive an arrow in the eye. The arrow, ill-aimed, rebounded from a stone and would certainly have hit me if I had not thrown myself flat. Moreover, the bow itself hardly satisfied me, for it bent less and less well, and became unusable. There must be a secret in bow-making. After many attempts, here is how I managed to make a proper bow. First, the choice of materials: I cut a lath out of a flexible wood which I dried to get rid of all dampness. I cut it to my own height, and I doubled its middle part with a piece of the same wood, well lashed on but curving naturally in the opposite direction. This tension forced my bow constantly to straighten itself. Instead of a simple liana, the cord is made from very tough goat-gut. My arrows are bamboo canes, on which I fix bone points or small triangles of forged iron. The feathering of my arrows has caused me much vexation, these little feathers are indispensable, however, for making the bolt fly straight to the mark. I arranged them so badly that they made my arrows fly astray at every shot. I have had to make a sketch to explain this irregularity to myself and correct my faulty placing. Then my bow shot straight, but it was so big and heavy that it hampered me in the under-growth, and made so much racket by breaking twigs and branches that the hunted animal escaped. I fashioned therefore a smaller bow, harder to bend but easier to hide. I made, as well, a quiver for the ten or twelve arrows I had completed. Then I had more troubles; the bow, though ac-curate, had a short range. So I built a crossbow. The day I returned from the hunt drag-ging behind me a peccary and two turkeys killed by the cross-bow was marked by a great feast, shared by Japp and Poll, and washed down by a pint of rum!

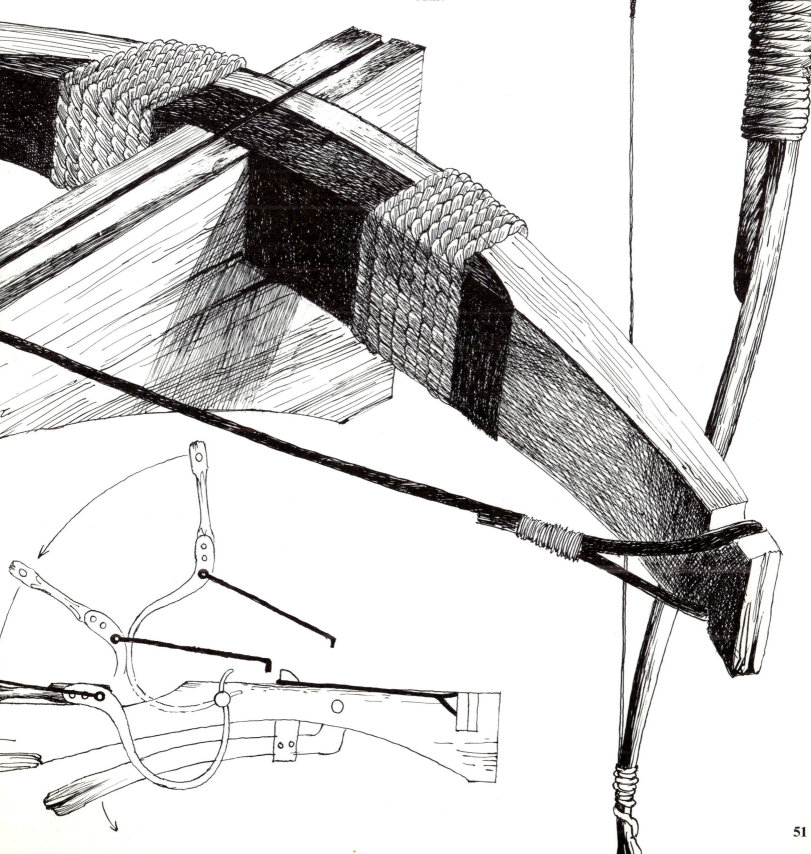

MARCH 1669/MY AVIARY

I always visit with pleasure the highest homes in my kingdom, I mean my tree cabins. Nevertheless, I do not gain the same benefit from them as of old. I am no longer so nimble, and, my isle having become familiar, I am less entertained by discovering this strange tree, that stream, or this herd of peccaries crossing a tobacco field. At present, birds above all hold my attention; I sketch them and pass long hours in observing their habits. I have caught some, and have caged them in a big aviary set up near the entrance to my cave. Toucans, above all, attract me with their enormous many-coloured beaks. I also have parrots and parakeets which I teach to speak and to whistle. The grindstone where I sharpen my knives is an excellent flute-master, and it is wonderful to hear the creaking song of the winch taken up by their nasal voices. Poll, my favourite parrot, speaks very well; that is, he repeats all day long: "Robin! Where are you? What are you saying? What are you doing? Poor Robin!" I reply to him: "Poll, my dear friend, I am sifting my flour! I am cutting wood! I am baking bread!" I have also two or three golden caurales strutting about and showing off, disdainful and royal, rare birds, and they brighten my lawn. With my tame kids, my farmyard, my old dog and my cats (I succeeded one day in attracting a wild cat who had her kittens in one of my baskets), I have always round me a crowd of animals to keep me company.

SURROUNDINGS OF
MY DWELLING,
FIFTEEN YEARS
AFTER MY ARRIVAL
ON THE ISLAND

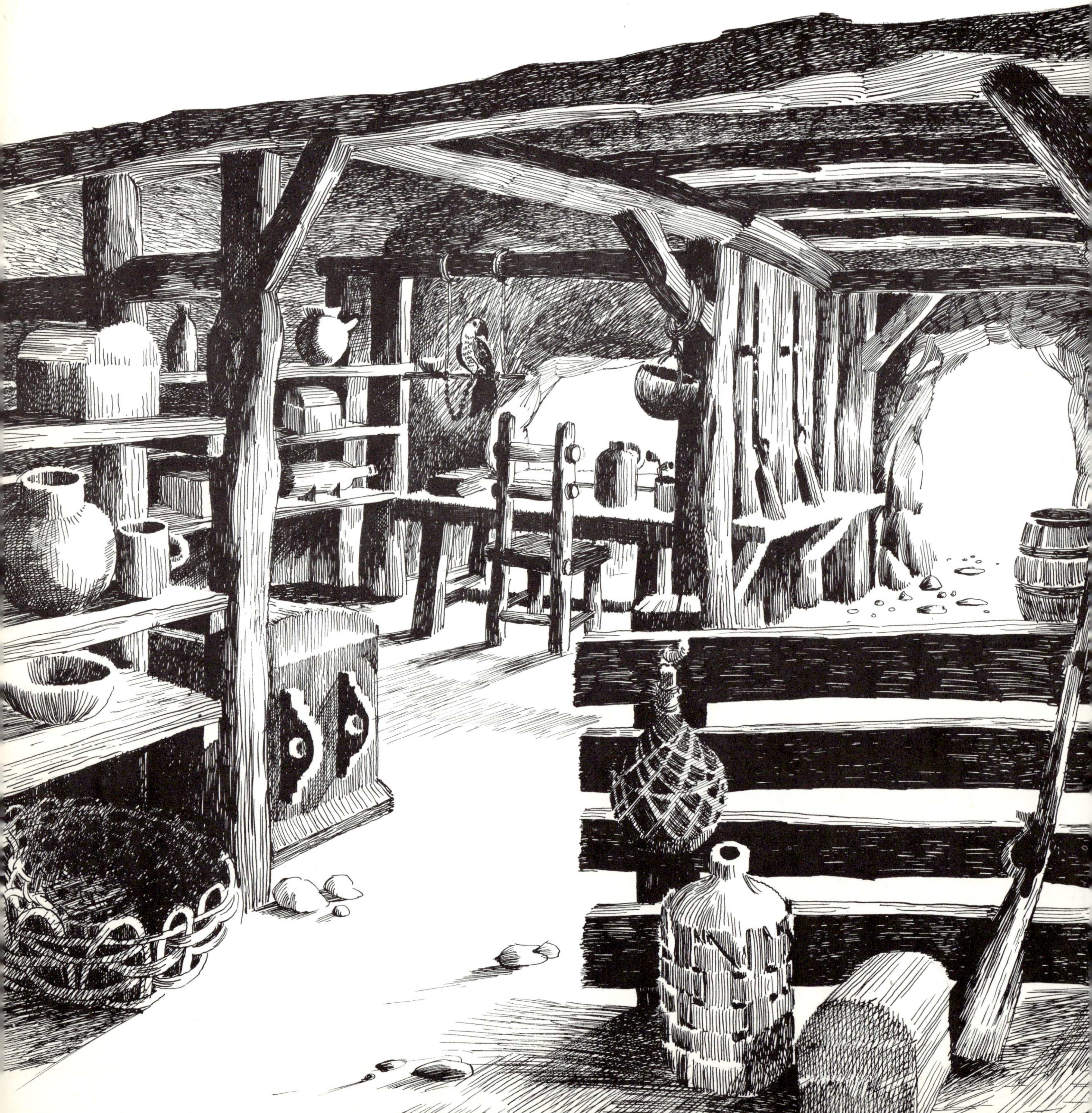

Quite a long time ago the wish to make a picture of my home first enticed me. Now that everything in it is arranged and set out to my fancy, I undertake its detailed description. First, the room where I live, read, draw, write, and play music. Then the corner where I sleep soundly in shelter, in a recess which I have hollowed out in the rock, raised, cushioned and covered with furs; finally the kitchen, which opens on my lawn. I have built a chimney whose flue finds its way out through a crack in the rock; it draws excellently when the wind is south-south-west; less well when it is in the opposite quarter. In that case I profit by it to smoke my fish and haunches of meat. This is the part of my dwelling that I first began to hollow out when the shelter was only a store for provisions and other things. It was this part that collapsed at the time of the earthquake, which very luckily has never occurred again, and I had to support it with beams and posts. Afterwards, I deepened it and installed my bed in it like a ship's bunk. Then, continuing my earthworks, I returned towards the cliff face, completing my dwelling by two fine openings towards the sun, for windows. My house is thus in the form of a U. To show it more clearly, I am busying myself in making a plan of my cave.

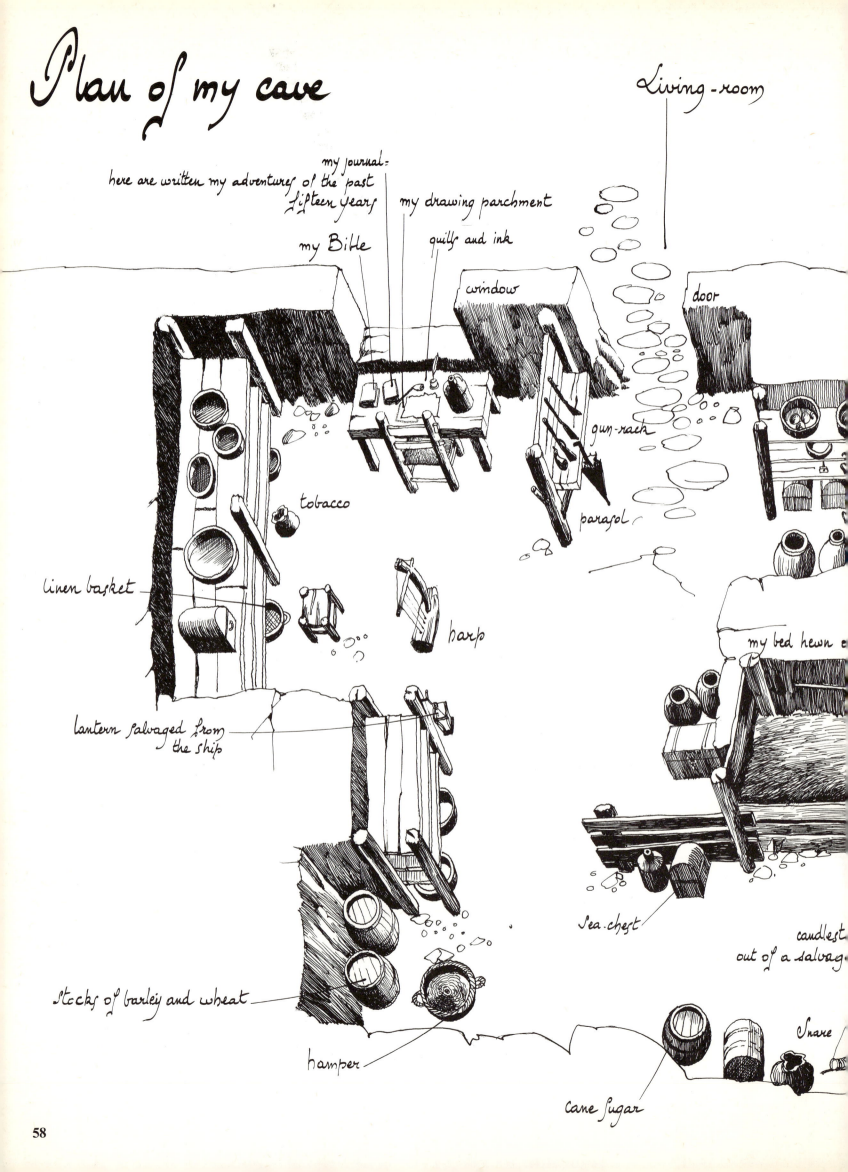

Plan of my cave

Living-room

here are written my adventures of the past
fifteen years

my journal—

my drawing parchment

my Bible

quills and ink

window

door

gun-rack

tobacco

parasol

linen basket

harp

my bed hewn

lantern salvaged from
the ship

Sea-chest

candlest
out of a salvag

Stocks of barley and wheat

hamper

Cane sugar

Snare

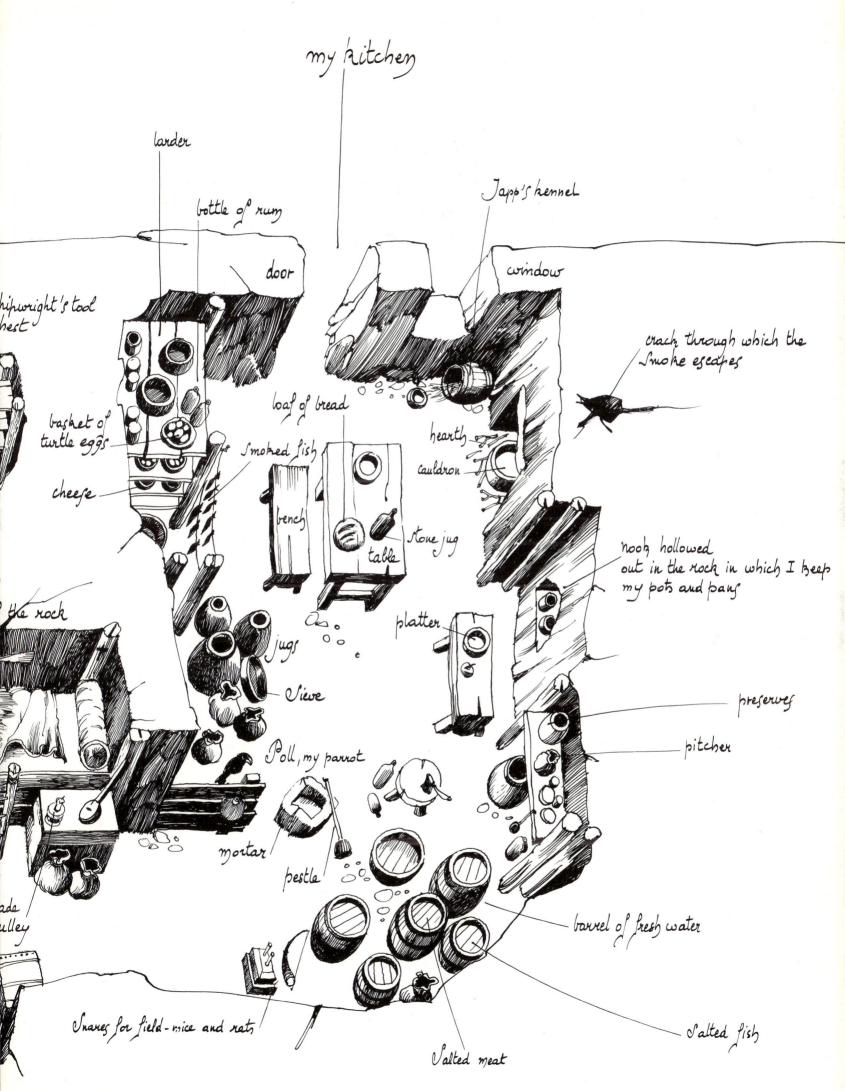

my kitchen

larder

bottle of rum

door

Japp's kennel

window

hipwright's tool chest

crack through which the smoke escapes

loaf of bread

basket of turtle eggs

smoked fish

hearth

cauldron

cheese

bench

the rock

jugs

table

stone jug

nook hollowed out in the rock in which I keep my pots and pans

sieve

platter

preserves

pitcher

Poll, my parrot

mortar

pestle

barrel of fresh water

ade ulley

Snares for field-mice and rats

Salted meat

Salted fish

DECEMBER 1675
THE RIVER IS IN FLOOD

I have just had an unfortunate accident. A whole load of wood intended for the enlargement of my enclosure has capsized into the river. I believe I have already said the crossing of this stream is very difficult in the rainy season. There are whirlpools, strong currents, treacherous rapids. In ordinary times, I use, at my own risk, a sort of barge, for transporting wood, charcoal, and salt. It also sometimes happens that a month passes without my being able to set foot on the other bank, which is very inconvenient. I am much vexed by this happening. It is curious to see how much I am affected by small incidents. It is not in itself the loss of the wood which bothers me, but the fact that sometimes nature, with whom I live in perfect harmony, shows herself hostile.

6 DECEMBER

This morning I have just returned from the place where the barge upset. Some tree trunks have slipped 10 feet lower and jammed themselves across the river, forming, indeed, almost the framework of a bridge. This, naturally enough, has given me the idea of strengthening this rickety collection and making it into a construction which can defy the seasons. I am no longer as in my first days here in terror of being surprised by attackers coming from the other side of the island. Nothing need prevent me from building a bridge. I will set the work in hand tomorrow.

7 DECEMBER 1675

I must be reasonable. These three logs will never make a bridge. Moreover, the season is too unfavourable for this project. I must wait for the dry months to start a stronger piece of work, and one better thought out, for in wishing to

hurry things on I run a great risk of being swept away and drowned by the angry flood. Let us wait.

11 AUGUST 1676

Victory! The bridge, which for so long I have promised myself to build, has been inaugurated today. Japp has crossed the river without wetting his paws. I followed him, solemnly, proud of my work, which I have christened "Robinson Crusoe Bridge".

SEPTEMBER* 1676
THE WORST DISAPPOINTMENT IN MY LIFE

For two hours I have believed that a ship was coming to my rescue, but alas, no . . . Here is how it happened. Yesterday morning a hurricane wind was sweeping the island, and I came, as every day, to climb up to my look-out post, hollowed in the upper face of my cliff, to search the horizon with my telescope. A white sail showed itself! Joy and anxiety at once assailed me violently. I came down again very quickly and made a great fire to signal my presence to the ship. The vessel seemed to be steered by a

drunken man, for it tacked, lost way, recovered; in short, it had a disabled air. At midday a great gust of wind made the ship lie over to the point of taking in water, then righted her and flung her fiercely against the reefs half a mile from the shore, where she broke up. I could not keep back a cry of despair. I saw two men launch the ship's boat and jump in. But the storm was so violent that she overturned and the two poor wretches drowned before my eyes. I could do

nothing for them. I cannot tell the extent of my horror at this tragedy. All afternoon I have watched to see if any life showed itself on board the wreck. There was nothing. The ship had held on all night, and in the morning it was gone. How can I express the depths of my disappointment? Fate has ordained that the only sail seen in seventeen years of my lonely life should be a ship just about to break up on the rocks of my island, at the very moment when I believed myself saved at last. To my mind, the crew, to have let the ship go adrift like that, must have been decimated by an epidemic, or annihilated by some tragedy of which I shall never hear.

*September: period at which tornadoes are frequent

Plan of my island

mangrove swamp

valley in which my country-house lies hidden

marsh where I collect my salt

North-Western point off which I was swept away by the currents

my tree-house

Robinson Crusoe bridge

tomb of my poor Japp

charcoal furnaces

tree in which I spent my first night on the island

N W E S

Rock onto which the ship was swept by the tide

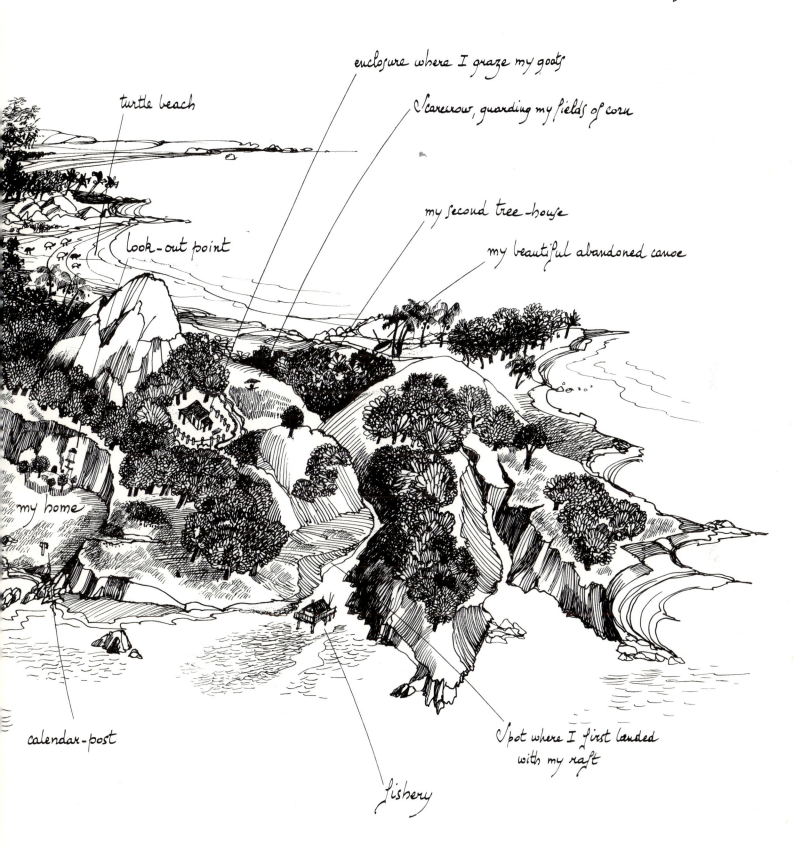

Terra Incognita

enclosure where I graze my goats

Scarecrow, guarding my fields of corn

turtle beach

my second tree-house

look-out point

my beautiful abandoned canoe

my home

calendar-post

Spot where I first landed
with my raft

fishery

Sand bank where the ship
was wrecked

**MAY 1678
JAPP LEAVES ME**

My life on the island flows placidly on. Nevertheless, these last days I have felt a very deep grief: Japp, at the end of his strength, having been for eighteen years my faithful companion in loneliness, died peacefully. His tomb is on the slope facing the sea.

MY FAVOURITE HOBBIES

Now that all my dispositions are finished, both in the interior of my dwelling and its surroundings, I can devote a little more time to leisure. My latest indulgence has been to make myself a new pipe. I had previously modelled one in earthenware, a little thick and clumsy but drawing very well. Then I patiently carved a stem in rosewood which I have fitted to a very thin bowl of earthenware. It is delightful to smoke in this pipe the aromatic tobacco I harvest twice a year.

I have taken also to music. Oh! I do not claim to charm an audience; I would be hard put to, and neither my kids nor my cats are going to complain of false notes. But it is a great happiness to me to break the evening silence by playing on the harp, the zither, or the panpipes, instruments created from empty gourds, wood, and strings of gut.

MY PRECIOUS SKETCHBOOKS

I have never ceased drawing since I came here, and I have now a very fine collection of pictures. I use goatskin dried and scraped so as to keep only a very flexible thin film of parchment. But it needs long and patient preparation. Naturally the pictures representing the shipwreck and the riches salvaged from the vessel, were drawn from memory much later.

I have used the captain's ink to the last drop, and when it gave out I was greatly distressed, looking at my empty bottle. But, one day, when fishing with a net, drawing out of the water some calamaries, a kind of cuttlefish, one of them furious, released a brownish-black liquid which soaked my feet.

I took care, afterwards, to collect these cuttlefish regularly and empty their pouches of the ink they contained. For quill pens, my farmyard supplies them abundantly, but it is the feathers of hoccos which are the finest and most flexible.

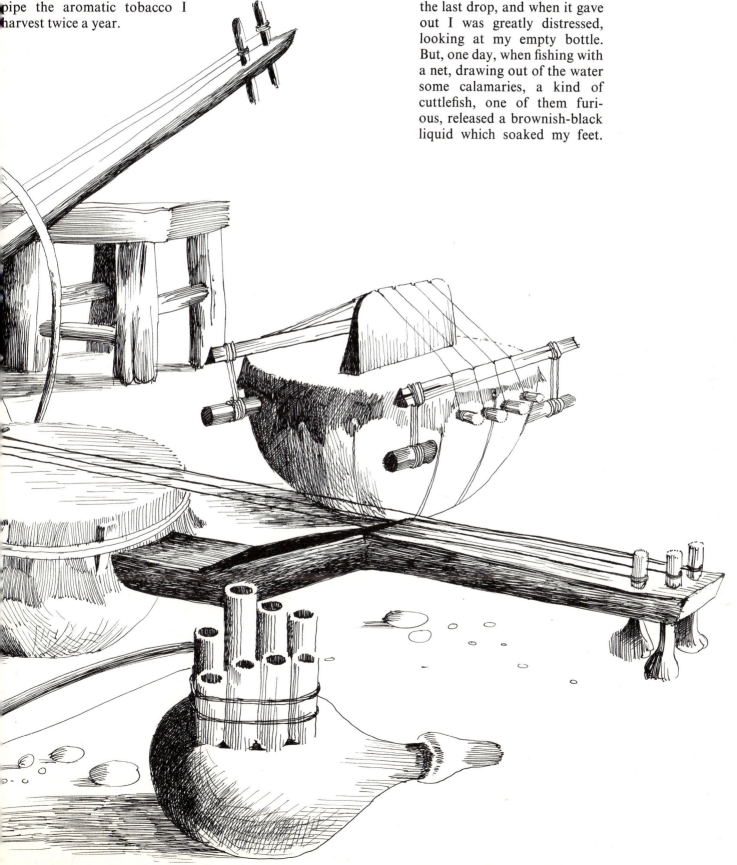

THE SECRET OF A SHIP IN A BOTTLE

One night recently, I had a strange dream. I dreamed I saw our poor three-master sailing proudly on the sea. The notion came to me to carve and rig a little ship in her likeness, and to put it in an empty brandy bottle with a wide neck.

How to get the ship into the bottle; that is a secret which I learned from an old fisherman. The masts and rigging must be laid flat on the hull before being inserted into the neck; then they are raised inside the bottle with the help of a draw-string. It needs ingenuity to get hold of all the materials, to wit: the bottle, first of all, soft wood to make the hull, fine rods of tough wood for the masts and spars. I have had to unravel cloth for threads, and to get brass wire, I have had to undo the strings of beads that our captain intended for the natives of Africa with whom we were going to trade. I have cut out the sails from the cloth of a shirt; I have stiffened them lightly with starch, and by setting them to dry on a round branch I have given them a fine swell, to simulate the wind in the sails. I made myself some fish glue, and I have even extracted gum from the gum-dragon tree to make the sea . . . in the bottle.

My tools? A small penknife, a scrap of razor, a small wood-chisel, a needle fixed in a handle whose bevelled point I use to pierce the masts and spars without breaking them; a pair of pincers, a long-handled hook, a palette knife, and metal rods.

HOW I CONSTRUCT MY BOAT OUTSIDE THE BOTTLE

I carve the hull, which I naturally make a little smaller than the bottle neck. I make a notch in it forward for fixing the bowsprit. I cut the masts, in the top of which I pierce a hole to pass a ring or loop through; I have made plenty of sketches to show details of this. Then I set the yards, as in the drawing, so that they can be placed parallel to the masts when the ship is put in the bottle. There are three yards on the foremast and the mizzen mast, four on the main mast. I drive the masts firmly into their positions. Now I place the thread which raises the rigging. A strong straining

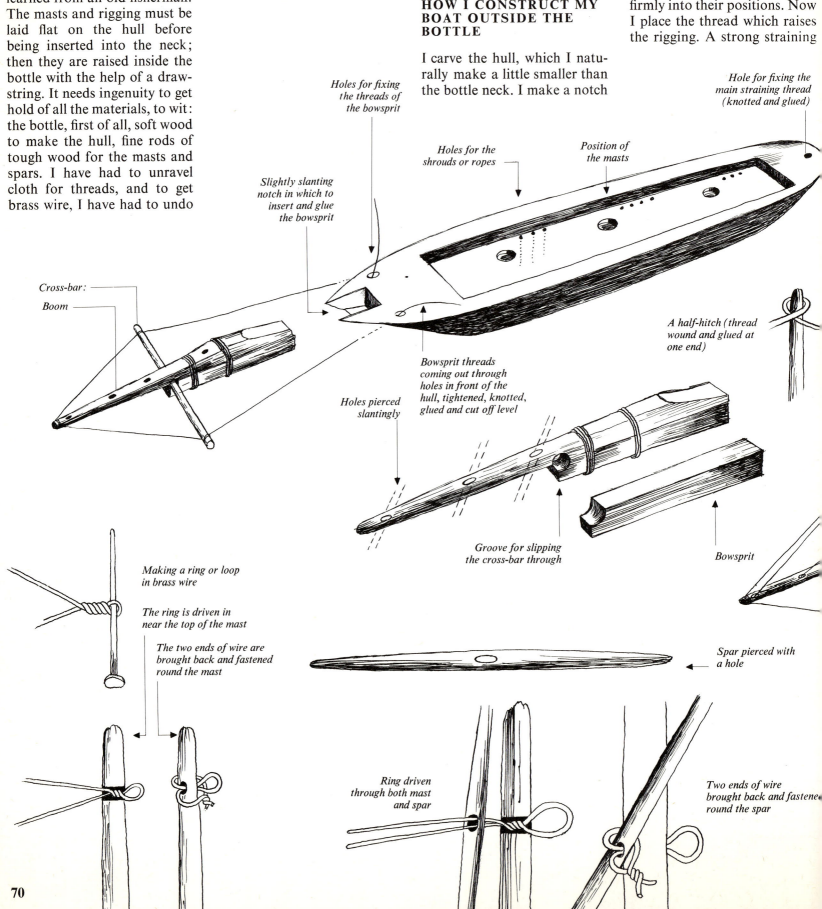

Holes for fixing the threads of the bowsprit

Holes for the shrouds or ropes

Position of the masts

Hole for fixing the main straining thread (knotted and glued)

Slightly slanting notch in which to insert and glue the bowsprit

Cross-bar:

Boom

A half-hitch (thread wound and glued at one end)

Bowsprit threads coming out through holes in front of the hull, tightened, knotted, glued and cut off level

Holes pierced slantingly

Groove for slipping the cross-bar through

Bowsprit

Making a ring or loop in brass wire

The ring is driven in near the top of the mast

The two ends of wire are brought back and fastened round the mast

Spar pierced with a hole

Ring driven through both mast and spar

Two ends of wire brought back and fastened round the spar

thread attached to the back of the hull fixes aloft the three masts by a half-hitch. The thread is wrapped round once and stuck, and then it comes to slip into the first hole of the boom. I put in position the stays of the foremast, which slip into the second, third, and fourth holes of the boom. These four threads are stretched and fixed temporarily by a nail holding the masts upright. I place the shrouds or ropes as I show them in the sketch, taking care to thread tiny beads at their bases to make the dead-eyes. The threads go through the hull and are knotted underneath. Next I place the tackle and the slings of the yards, that is, the threads which hold the yards to the masts, and which by running through the rings or shackles allow them to pivot. This work demands great care, for it is important not to go wrong.

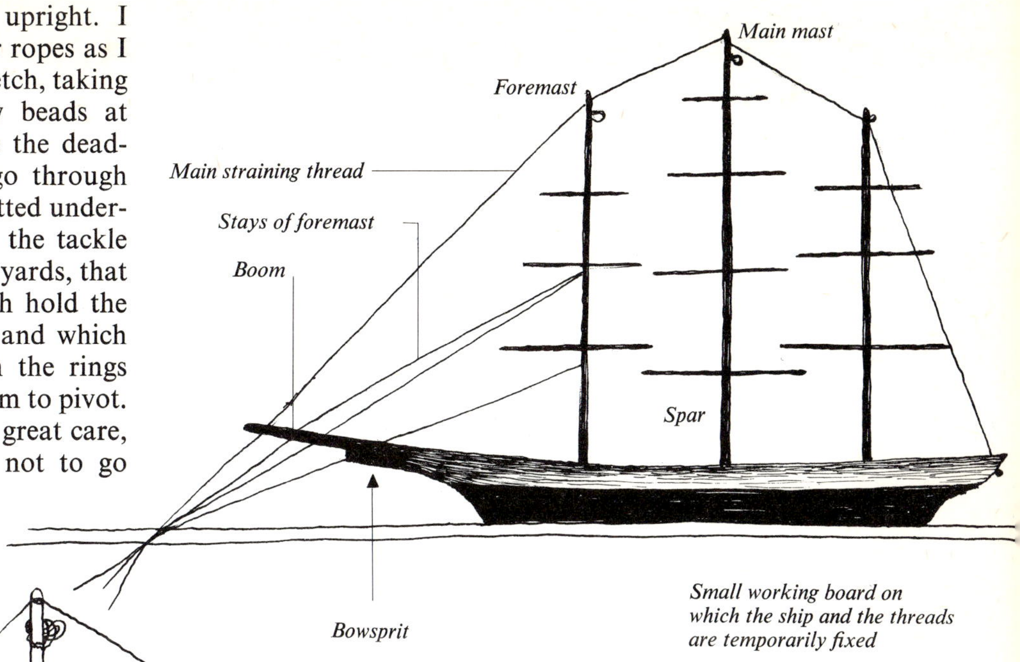

Main mast

Foremast

Main straining thread

Stays of foremast

Boom

Spar

Bowsprit

Small working board on which the ship and the threads are temporarily fixed

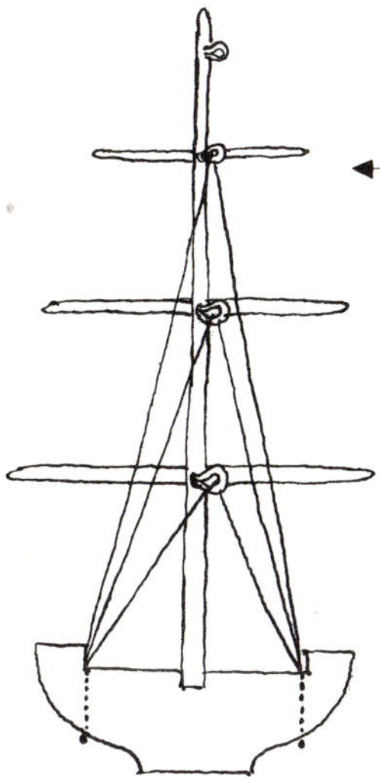

The shrouds or ropes are made with threads passing through the ring of each spar, then through the holes in the hull to come out and be knotted under the hull

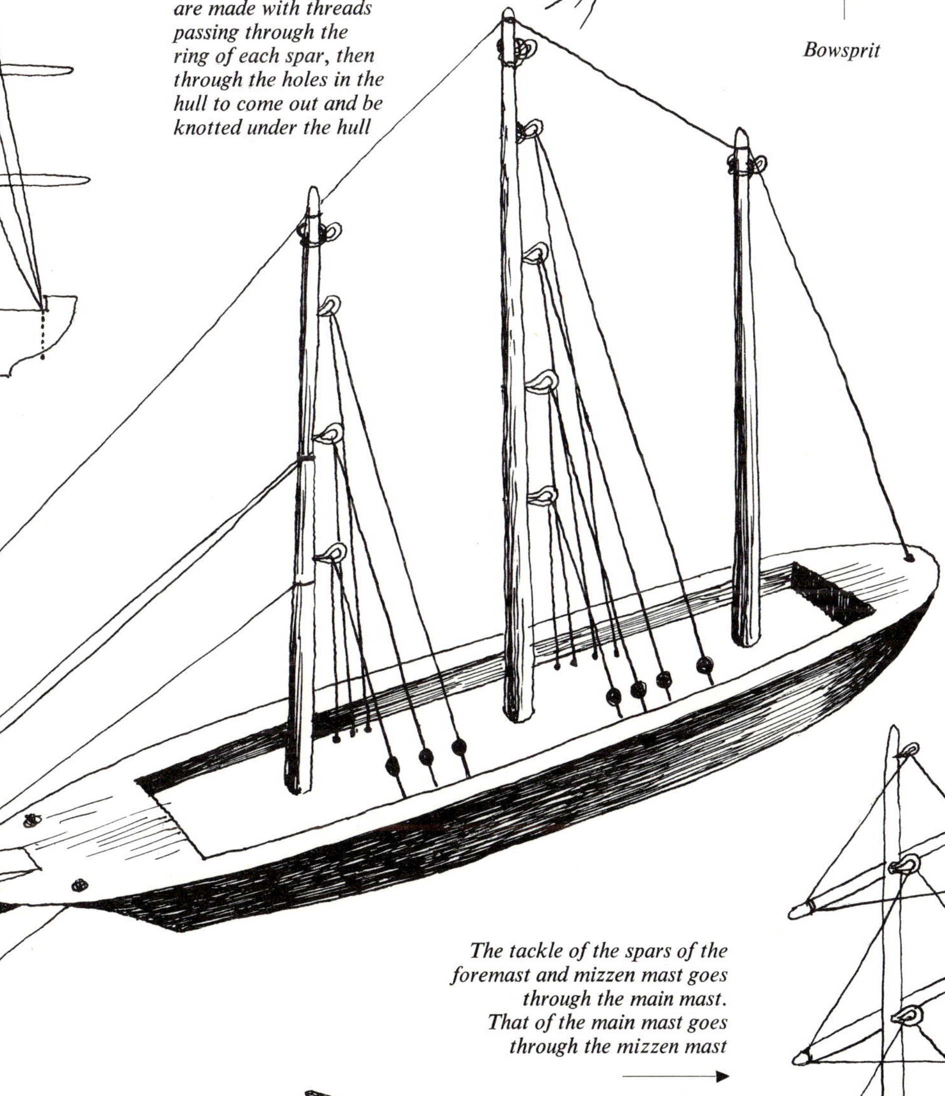

You can thread and knot small beads to make the deadeyes at the base of the shrouds

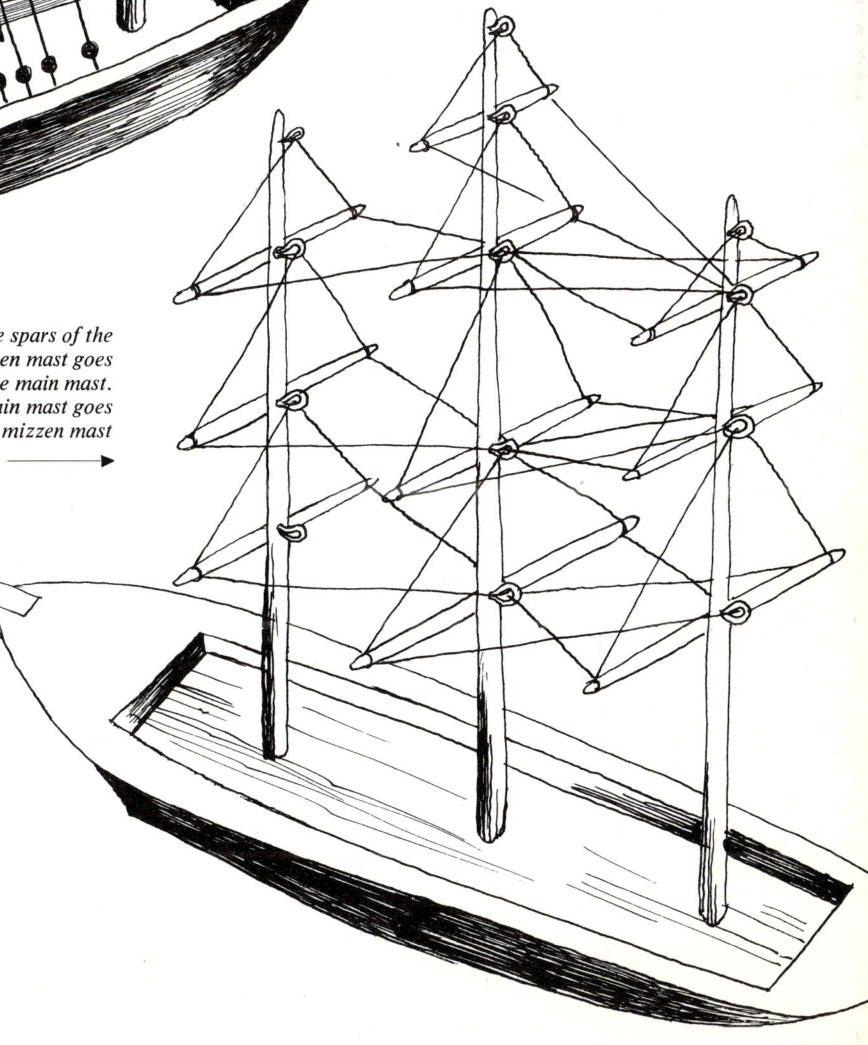

The tackle of the spars of the foremast and mizzen mast goes through the main mast. That of the main mast goes through the mizzen mast

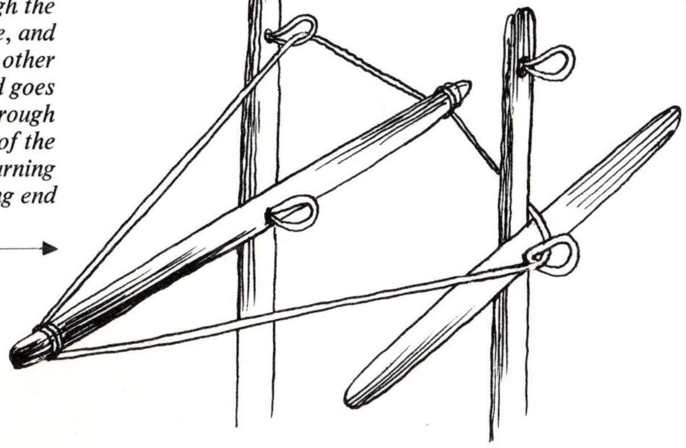

Placing of the tackle and slings of the spars. The rolled and glued thread (half-hitch) at the end of the spar passes through the ring in the mast, above, and then is fastened on the other end of the spar, and goes on to be threaded through the ring on the spar of the next mast before returning be fixed on the starting end

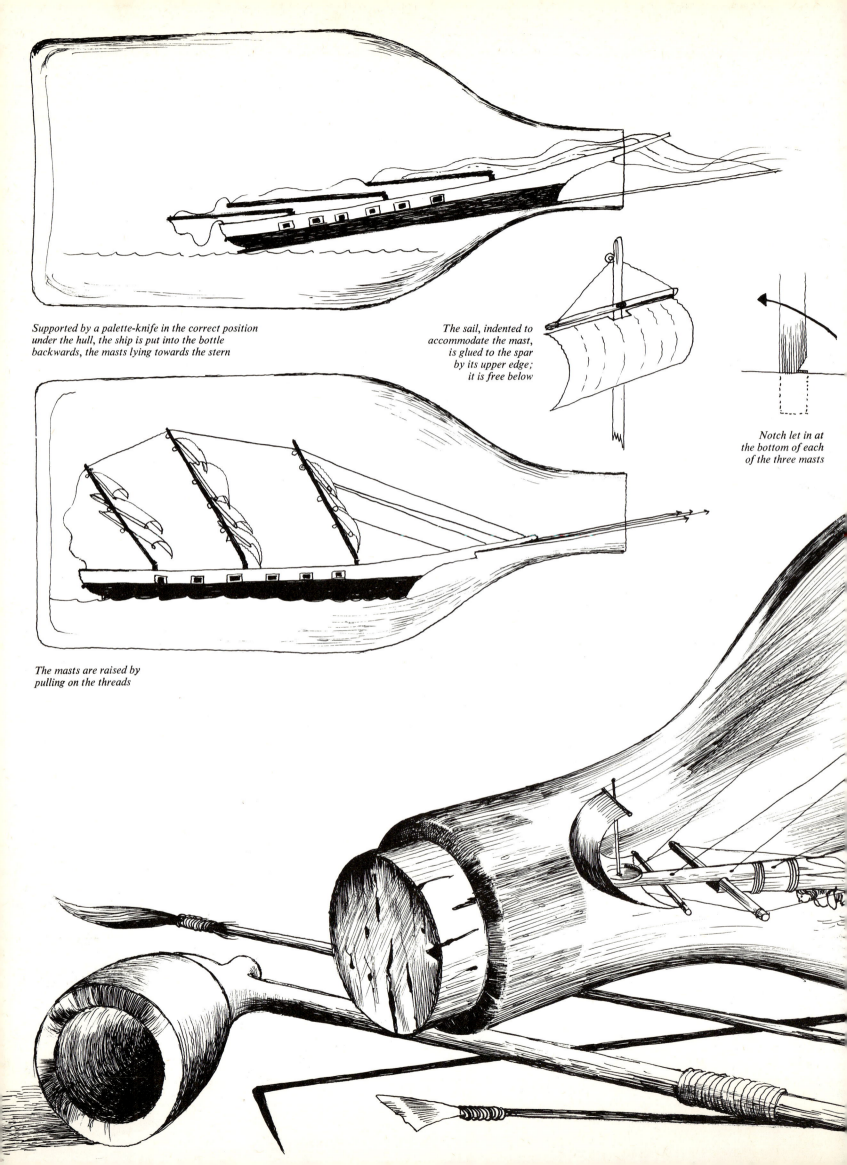

Supported by a palette-knife in the correct position under the hull, the ship is put into the bottle backwards, the masts lying towards the stern

The sail, indented to accommodate the mast, is glued to the spar by its upper edge; it is free below

Notch let in at the bottom of each of the three masts

The masts are raised by pulling on the threads

HOW I FOLD THE SHIP

Finally, I glue the sails under the yards by their top edges only. Now I make at the base of each mast a little notch level with the deck, I release the straining-threads, and I delicately lay the masts down backwards, taking great care not to break them. I arrange the spars parallel to the masts; the ship is quite flat and ready to be inserted into the bottle. I should say here that I had previously poured into the bottle lying on its side some gum, now solidified, in which I had provided a groove to hold the well-glued keel of the hull. This gum is reddish; I am original; I have a red sea! But no matter. Next I glue the keel, and I gently push the ship, masts forward, through the neck of the bottle, holding the bowsprit as long as possible. Guiding it with the palette-knife, I place the ship in the groove and leave it there for a full day and a night.

AT LAST! THE GREAT DAY ARRIVES!

By pulling on the straining-strings and the stays, I raise the masts again to the vertical. I keep the main thread held by a nail driven into the small board which acts as a mount. With a long-handled hook, I replace the yards across the masts, I spread the sails, and put all in good order. Only then do I fix the straining-threads permanently. For that, taking pincers, I place a drop of glue in the spot where the thread comes out of the boom: I wait until the thread is well stuck, then, with the help of a very sharp blade fixed in a long handle, I cut the thread at the level of the wood. I do the same for the three other threads.

It remains only to decorate my vessel. I put the tiller in place, the figure-head on the prow (a little figure representing Hope), the anchor, a ship's bell, a small boat, cleats, ship's lanterns, and a top-gallant sail on the bowsprit. All but the sail are delicately carved in wood, decorated in ink and stuck on the deck. To do this I take the long sharpened hook, I pick up each object, previously well glued, I put it in its place, and I detach the hook, holding the object down meanwhile with a long rod. And there is my ship finished. I carefully recork the bottle. I must acknowledge that with patience and ingenuity I have succeeded in making a little masterpiece.

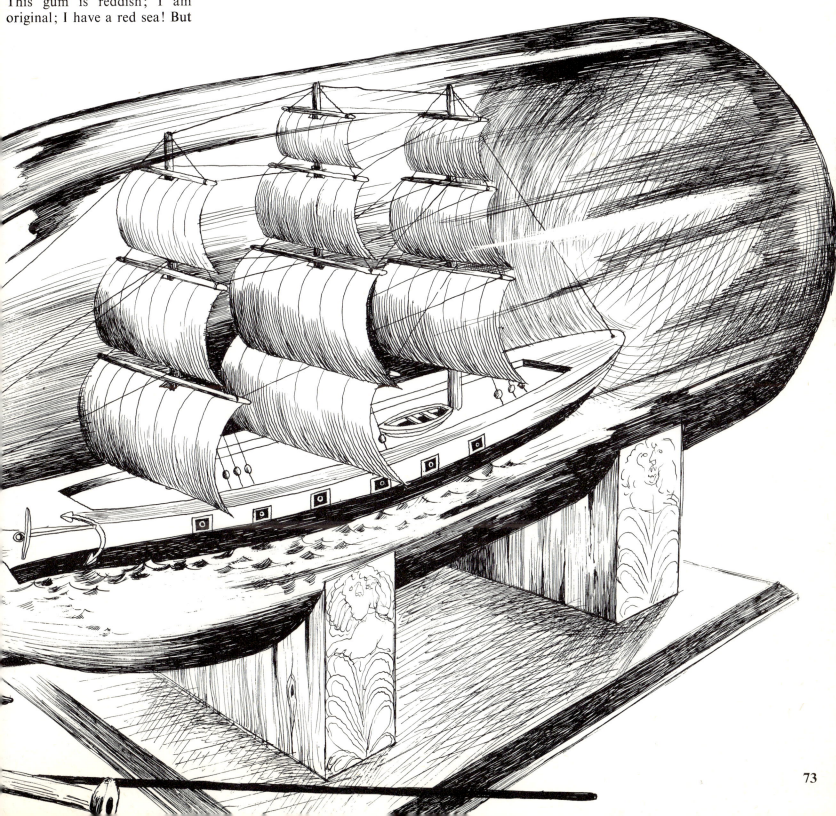

... I shall finish this picture as I was drawing the ... turtle, I saw something so alarming that I ran home and locked myself in. I shall not move from here for a long time, for in the sand, two paces away from my bottle of ink, I saw the imprint of a naked foot! God help me! I am no longer alone on this island!

January 3rd 1680

24 JANUARY 1680
THREE AGONIZING WEEKS

Three weeks have passed since I saw in the sand the undeniable sign of the assault of my kingdom by the unknown, I mean the footprint. Three weeks during which I have racked my mind to know from whence the footprint came; three weeks that I have passed shut up in my cave, only daring to go to my meadow at nightfall, so that three of my best milking goats have fallen ill. Yesterday I buried one of them that had just died. What a horrible state to be in! I do not go to the river, I cut no wood. I have tried to reassure myself by saying that the footprint was my own, but I never walk barefoot on the burning sand of the beach, for a very good reason, from the time when, stung by a huge spider, I was feverish for two days in the summer of the year 1674.

No! All things considered, a man, a savage, must have landed on this island. He lives here perhaps with his whole tribe. They will certainly find out my retreat, and then all will be up with Robinson Crusóe.

JULY 1680

Six months have passed by since I wrote these last words. I cannot think of this period of my life without deep sorrow. "Poor Robin" Poll repeats again and again. I was within an ace of going mad. One day, it was fifteenth June, I took my guns, my pistols, two sabres, a strong cutlass, and, determining to sell my life dearly, I returned to the turtle beach, crossing the island from one side to another. The state of my orchard, of my fields, of my dairy-farm, rent my heart as I passed them. All was left to ruin. But I must confess that I saw nothing, absolutely nothing, which betrayed another human presence on the island. Had I dreamed it all? I returned to the spot where I had seen the footprint. Protected from the wind by a big stone, less clear perhaps, the footprint was still there. I returned home less disheartened, for I had been able to search the neighbourhood and to convince myself that no other trace had been left, apart from those of hundreds of turtles which live on this shore.

I take up my life again as in the past, with the sole difference that I never go out to pick a citron or to fetch a pitcher of water without having my artillery on my back. Ended the walks, finished the sketches, gone the long hours of dreaming or sleeping in the grass!

5 FEBRUARY 1681
AN EXTRAORDINARY EVENT

It is night, I am writing by the light of a candle. Everyone is asleep: cats, birds, hens, kids, but mixed with these animal exhalations are those of a man, an Indian, who sleeps two paces from me, worn out by his terrifying adventure. I do not know if tomorrow he may not attempt to kill me. However, the poor devil has a fear-stricken air, and seems to feel for me a touching gratitude. Who can tell?

Here is what has passed: a year has rolled by since my first terrors, and I have almost forgotten the footprint. Yesterday I went out at midday to look for turtles' eggs on the coco-palm beach. I am very partial to these eggs cooked in the ashes. The moment I came out of the wood, a sound of paddles striking the water alerted me. I threw myself flat on my face behind a rock; savages were just landing from a canoe. There sprang out of it four, five, six, ten men, all with fierce aspects and wearing horrifying masks and feathers on their heads. Two of them started to make a fire, while two others dragged from the canoe a poor bound mortal. They threw him on the ground, and, horrible, killed him with a hatchet. Then they went to drag out a second man, quite young, who with a single leap knocked over his butchers and began to run and run, pursued by two shouting savages. The unfortunate soul seemed to fly, sustained by fear, and I watched. Oh, God, he is coming towards me! What shall I do? They will catch him! I seized my gun and aimed at the first pursuer. At the shot, the man reeled and fell dead at a stroke. The other, in the height of terror, half-turned. The fugitive stopped, bewildered, saw the man stretched out, and boldly went over to touch him. It was at this moment that I appeared with my gun smoking in my hand. The young savage threw himself down in an attitude of supplication. I concluded from this that my appearance must be formidable. Seeing that the savages were trying to regroup, I reloaded, and fired in their direction and hit two of them. The others then sprang into their canoe, taking their wounded, and fled, paddling with all their might.

The young savage trembled with fear and gazed at my guns and the body of his enemy with so striking an appearance of incomprehension that I burst out laughing. The youth also laughed, and threw himself at my feet, lifting his arms. I had to raise him to stop his demonstrations of submission. I made a sign to him to follow me, and he trod in my footsteps. We reached my country house. He rolled his eyes in surprise. When an agouti ran out under our feet I shot the beast, and it jumped away before falling dead in the grass. I signed to the Indian to look for it, and could not keep from smiling to see with what precautions he approached it. His admiration for me was confirmed, and while we were going towards my cave, he gave frequent looks at the agouti and at my gun. When we arrived at my castle, his astonishment was at its height. I gave him bread, one or two eggs, and a grapefruit. Then, showing him a corner where there were some rugs, I made a sign to him to lie down to sleep, which he would not do without having first thanked me again with childlike gestures.

6 FEBRUARY 1681
HE IS CALLED FRIDAY

I woke up this morning having fallen asleep with my nose in my diary. The young savage had disappeared. My mind was filled with thoughts of fear, treachery, grief at having perhaps lost a companion; but also joy at being still alive when my guest had had all possible chances to kill me in my sleep. As I finished rigging myself out with guns and sabres, fearing a sudden attack, there came from beyond my palisade a cheerful song and a call. I quickly went out, and saw the youth jump briskly over the fence, and run joyfully towards me, his hands filled with fruit. I smiled at him and made a welcoming gesture, because at my warlike aspect he had recoiled sharply. But I soon made him feel at home, and, throwing himself again on the ground, he placed my foot on his bent head, which seemed to indicate that he considered himself my slave. I raised him, and undertook at once to teach him a few words. I named him "Friday", for the day on which I rescued him. This appeared to please him greatly.

10 MAY 1681
FRIDAY'S STORY

For almost three months we have been together as good companions, Friday and I. I questioned him at length on the dramatic circumstances of his arrival on the island, and he explained it to me in very primitive English, and with many gestures. His nation had had to make war on an enemy people come to invade their territory. During the fight he was captured and put with another prisoner in a hut, from which he was dragged at the end of three days, to be thrown with his companion into a canoe. He knew all too well what fate awaited him at the end of the voyage: it was death, and more horrible still, the certainty that his body would be eaten by his captors. So while at sea, he succeeded in breaking his bonds, and when the canoe reached the island he jumped onto the beach and escaped.

I was horrified by this story, for I concluded from what he told me that the beach had often been the scene of these cruel practices. How many times, moreover, had I traversed these parts, or even surveyed them from the height of my watchtowers, without ever suspecting anything! What miracle saved me from being seen by these cannibal tribesmen? Without any doubt, it was due to the fact that I went only very rarely to this far coast of the island, and at periods presumably when the cannibals had not landed there, because of winds, or currents. This strengthened my determination never to set foot on that coast again, and I forbade Friday to venture there either. The poor lad, trembling again with fright, very willingly gave me his promise. I withheld however from our rather confused conversation that the footprint which had so much terrified me had indeed been that of a savage, come to partake of one of those horrible feasts. And that, not far from my island, were lands near enough for savage men to risk launching forth on the sea in such light canoes.

SECOND PLAN OF ESCAPE

Why should I not make with Friday's help a new attempt at escape in my beautiful canoe? He would serve as guide and interpreter, essential to keep us from falling into the hands of his tribal enemies. This project haunted me all night, and next day, armed to the teeth, accompanied by Friday, now formidable with my bow on his back, a cutlass in his belt, and carrying a club he had made himself, we went towards the creek where I had abandoned my canoe. Alas! We found her half rotted away. Twenty-one years had passed since her making. I decided then and there to build another.

JULY 1681
MY SECOND CANOE

We have begun making the canoe. First of all we cut down a very beautiful cedar tree, lopped off the branches, and trimmed it, and, following the advice of my young companion, we rolled it in the rough state as far as the sea.

4 MAY 1684

My fears are not revived by the idea of this voyage, for I shall be guided by Friday, who has already sailed it. I have stitched together a sail out of the scraps of those which I still have. It is a very fine square sail . . .
Ho! Friday is calling me! Good heavens, how alarmed he seems! What is happening?

4 MAY, EVENING
AT LAST!

I am scarcely restored from a fainting-fit. Doubtless from too much joy. I do not know how to write these words. I would rather shout them out, springing like a young goat. Friday does not hold back from dancing and singing. I was so carried away that I remained for a long time voiceless and silent in front of the worthy ship's captain who landed this afternoon near our beach. Here is how it came to pass. On hearing Friday shouting: "Master, a sail! Master, a ship!" I rushed to my ladders and climbed to my look-out point. With my spyglass I clearly saw a three-master tacking about, but unlike the other poor vessel this one was steered by a sure hand. I shouted to Friday to bring me up logs and brushwood, and I lighted a brazier which I covered with grass to make plenty of smoke. This succeeded beyond my hopes, and I even had to come down very quickly from my perch to avoid being smoked like a ham. At the start of the afternoon the proud ship, flying English colours, was anchored at some cable-lengths, and a longboat with six men on board landed on my beach. The captain jumped to the ground and, seeing me, stood still. I saluted him with these words: "Welcome to this island, Sir. I am an English subject and my name is Robinson Crusoe."

Then I had the immense joy of hearing a deep voice with a Liverpool accent answer me: "How are you, Sir?" And he held out his hand.

6 MAY
GOOD-BYE, MY ISLAND!
SHALL I NOT MISS YOU?

I have finished my preparations. Yesterday I went all over the island with the captain, to show him my property. His exclamations of surprise and admiration alternated with words of compassion and comfort which went straight to my heart. The captain having invited me to pass the night on board, we parted early.
I have set free the goats, cats, and birds. I have shut up my houses, not without great sorrow. I have kept as souvenirs my goatskin clothes, my cap and my umbrella, which I have packed in the bottom of a chest. I have rolled my sketchbooks in a piece of canvas. The longboat is afloat. Friday is already on board. I take my parrot on my shoulder. Good-bye, my island, good-bye!

7 MAY 1684
ON BOARD THE
THREE-MASTER
"JOLLY PRIZE"

The order is given to get under way. It is seven o'clock in the morning. In my journal I write these last words:
Today, the seventh May 1684, I, Robinson Crusoe, once master and sole inhabitant of a lost island, here bring to an end my sketchbooks and my journal, in which for almost a quarter of a century I have told and pictured my strange adventures. May the story of my fortunes set dreaming those who have the soul of a wanderer.

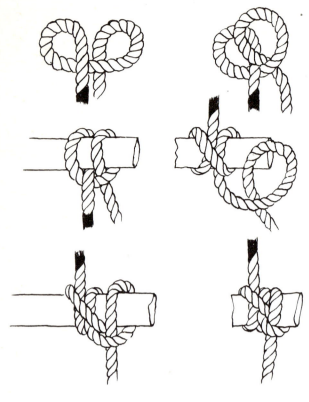

Clove hitch:
used in making rope ladders

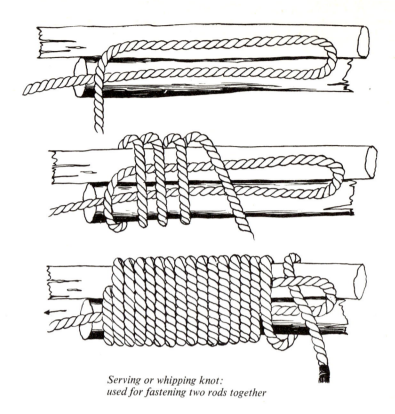

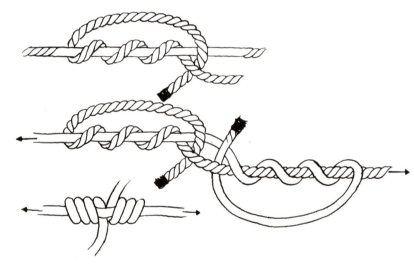

Serving or whipping knot:
used for fastening two rods together

Diamond knot: used for preventing
a rope from unravelling

Carrick bend:
used for tying two ropes together

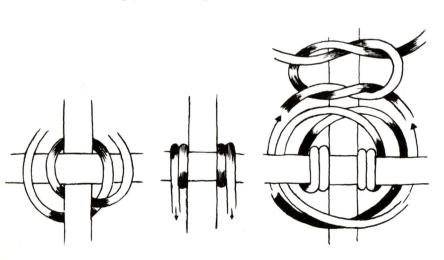

Lashing knot:
used for joining two crossing spars

Bowline:
used for non-running loop

INDEX